LIFE TAKER

The Story of the Gun

DANIEL CARLSON

Chapter 1

May 16th, 1861

"Drink up, my dear brother, for tomorrow you will lead the Republic into glory and confine the Union to a fable in the pages of the history books." David Vandehoff smiled and raised his glass of bourbon in the direction of his older brother, General Harden Vandehoff. Then he toasted, "To a speedy and sacrifice-restricted resolution."

"I do not share your optimism, Davy, and I fear your confidence is misjudged," the general replied. A veteran of the Mexican War, Harden Vandehoff had served as a colonel in the Battle of Palo Alto, and his memories had been forever impacted and scarred by the horrors inflicted upon the battlefield.

"Nonsense, Harden. Within months, you will have led the men of the South to a glorious victory and independence from the iron fist of the North." David's voice was cast in a low tone due to the potency of his brother's favourite bourbon, which burnt the inner tissues of his throat as he swallowed the libation.

"I fear you underestimate the resources of the North." The general turned away from the extravagant ballroom to look out of the window and across the huge grounds of his plantation.

A city of canvas Sibley tents could be seen in the darkness, and masses of silhouetted figures congregated around the many campfires.

There was no moon on this cloudy, dull night to illuminate either the grey uniforms or the soldiers' enthusiastic faces.

The general failed to hear the polka being played to his rear as his thoughts became occupied with the impending slaughter of the young, the fiddle players, the cooks, the gamblers, and the many other darkened figures of his army which had encamped themselves under the large majestic oak trees that lined his vast estate.

"I admit the strength of the North is buoyed by their wealth, but they have a distinct weakness for leaders and fighting men. You know only too well all the best cadets at West Point were from the South."

Harden did not respond to his brother's assumption.

"Oh, Lincoln will soon be running back to Congress with his tail well and truly clipped. He is then sure to be ousted as the Union seeks an immediate reconciliation with the superior South."

David paused, but only to drain the remnants of his glass. "That will be the end for the absurd plug hatter. It will be back to a lawyer's office in the middle of nowhere for him before he knows it. You mark my words, Harden."

A male servant approached and refilled David's empty glass. Harden placed the flat of his hand across his glass to decline the refreshment, and the servant withdrew himself to an unlit corner of the large room.

David Vandehoff stepped forward and stood beside his brother at the window to admire the sprawling detachment. "This conflict needs leaders like you, my brother, and you stand shoulder to shoulder alongside the best this army has to offer."

Again, Harden did not reply. His face creased with the age-induced lines of worry as he released an anxious smirk.

"I'm envious of you, Harden." This time, David's comment stirred a response.

"This is not an army, Davy. It is a collection of hardy thieves, beggars, labourers, rustlers, scoundrels, gallows dodgers, and malcontents from all walks of life."

"Nevertheless, with your patience, guidance, and leadership, they will fight with all the venom of the South combined. They will bring you great victories." David smiled and again offered a small toast. "Oh, I wish I had been issued a rank of your stature," he confessed.

"You overestimate my importance, Davy." Harden now turned away from the window to scan across the ballroom.

At the far end of the large rectangular room, the double doors were now closed and the smell of the hot roast had dissipated as the fine dining had been devoured.

He knew behind the barrier his house servants were busily restoring order and clearing away the scraps from the remains of the lavish feast which had been organised by Clara Vandehoff, the plantation mistress and the general's wife.

The meal and ball had been carefully planned so the antebellum patriarchal society of Mississippi could honour the local general and express their gratitude for leading their neighbours and their kin to victory against the enemy of the North, which had vowed to exterminate their livelihoods.

In front of the general, the majority of the assembled were adhering to Southern etiquette and engaging in a waltz as the band played out the remaining notes of the Grand March.

"Leading men to victory is to be envied."

"Leading men to their deaths cuts deep on a man's conscience, and many lives will be lost when we venture deep into the Union's lair."

"Yes, Harden. Lives will be lost, but long-lasting valour and dignity will be established."

"You know, Davy, the saddest thing to losing a battle is winning one."

The foreseen loss of lives burdened Harden's joviality, and he was not enjoying the evening's conviviality.

"This country is a nation of brothers, all of whom believe they are fighting for the right causes. It is going to be a long struggle between intelligence and physical force," he said.

"Oh, Harden. Stop being so melancholy and take my hand." Clara Vandehoff had noticed her husband's poignancy, and she sought to lighten his mood. "Come, come, let's dance."

She held out her arm in perfect timing with the band's opening salvo of 'The Battle Cry of Freedom'. She stretched out and offered her small hand, fully expecting her husband to comply with her request and fulfil his dutiful obligation in front of the esteemed audience.

To all-round smiles, the couple stepped to the centre of the glossy wooden floor, paused briefly to attain the correct dancing posture, then smiled and unleashed themselves with perfectly timed swirls and steps.

General Harden Vandehoff looked every part the leader of men. He was tall, with a straight long back and wide shoulders which filled his immaculate uniform perfectly.

Flashes of grey near his temples seemed to sparkle out from his neat black groomed pompadour as he twirled across the ballroom.

"Davy doesn't mean to upset you. He is proud of you, that's all, and you should humour him."

"He is an ignoramus lacking all reality."

"Please, Harden. Revel in tonight's frivolities and leave the trepidation for the morning."

He smiled agreeably into his wife's pale and unblemished face. She revelled in the adulation which the local capitalists bestowed upon her husband, and this pride was expressed in the radiance of her charm, yet she openly displayed humility.

Standing less than five feet tall, with her petite frame enveloped by a bottle-green taffeta gown, Clara looked many years younger than her thirty-five years of age.

Harden was conscious of his wife's beauty and tonight, as he stared deep into her jet-coloured eyes, he knew her elegance and warmth beamed throughout the whole ballroom and the eyes of the contingent were focused upon her and not him. He liked it this way. He could not match her Southern allure and grace, and he felt clumsy as he tried to match her careful dainty steps.

The music stopped and heads bowed, but the general's relief was short-lived as the band burst straight into *Darling Nellie Grey*, and Clara quickly took another firm grip of his hand to fling him straight into the new dance routine.

"Albert Malloy does not know how to behave in a ballroom," Clara whispered into Harden's ear as they watched him awkwardly bump from one couple to another.

"No, my dear, he does not, but what's truly important is that he knows how to behave on the field of battle," Harden replied, darting a welcoming glance of acknowledgement and a smile to his clumsy colonel.

"Please do not let any harm come to young Holmes," Clara asked as they turned and faced an excitable young couple. "I couldn't bear to see Maisy wearing black before she's had the chance to wear white."

Harden spun Clara around and out of everyone's earshot. He whispered, "I'll reassign him as soon as we set pace."

Now assured, Clara relaxed and enjoyed the remainder of the dance, which to her disappointment was prematurely ended when David Vandehoff stood in front of the band and started to tap loudly on a glass decanter.

The music slowly ceased and silence almost befell the room.

"Ladies and gentlemen, friends and family of the South," he hailed. "May I have your attention for one moment please. Tomorrow morning my brother, General Harden Vandehoff, will lead out the great army of Mississippi to confront our enemy." Instant applause sounded. "Within weeks our loved ones will be upon the lands of the Northern oppressors and in direct armed combat with Winfield Scott's blue bellies."

Silence had now fully descended and concerned glances were flicked between the ladies, whilst looks noting excitable cravings for adventure mantled the faces of the men at their sides.

David clicked his thumb with his fingers and signalled with a nod to one of the male servants.

"General Vandehoff, can you step forward, please?" David held out his hand as an invitation. "On behalf of the citizens of Lawrence County, I would like to present you with this special gift."

The servant handed David a highly polished wooden box.

"To a very rare and special leader, may I present you with this truly unique gift to show our appreciation and gratitude," David said, handing the box to his smiling, but embarrassed, older brother.

Applause resonated around the room again as Harden deliberately placed the heavy walnut box on a table in front of him. He bowed his head and nodded to acknowledge the recognition.

As the noise dimmed, the click of the lock could be heard as he raised the two brass retaining latches which secured the lid. Harden slid his hand carefully across the smooth dark case and slowly raised the lid.

A bright reflection flashed and emblazoned briefly on his gracious face as he raised the lid to reveal a silver-plated LeMat revolver.

He maintained an arched position over the table as he gazed at the weapon of destruction. Everyone in the room remained silent as they watched him carefully raise the gun from the green baize mould. His nostrils filled with the scent of fresh walnut as he balanced the weight of the piece delicately across the flat of his hand.

He lifted the gun closer to his eyes and marvelled as he studied the elaborate floral engravings on the silver. He turned over the gun and lipped the serial number, '428'.

David watched his brother's face reveal his admiration for the weapon and saw him mouth out the numbers.

"428 is a very rare collectible. General Beauregard has 427 and our friend General Braxton Bragg has 429," David disclosed.

Harden finally raised his head to face the assembly. "I do not know what to say. Seems a shame to take it out of the box."

"Harden, this ain't no ornament. She will serve you well," David asserted.

"Indeed, she will." Harden replied as he read the engraved message inside the box lid.

'To General Vandehoff. A husband, a dear friend and a leader of the South. With great appreciation, love, and respect. From the citizens of Lawrence County.'

"I am too lost for words to express my gratitude for this splendid gift," he confessed with a hint of a glaze in his eyes.

"We can't have a war without weapons, so just whip arse those God darn Yankees and send fat old Winfield Scott hightailing it back to Washington!" someone shouted out as applause and laughter erupted.

"And we can't have a ball without music! Come! Dance, everyone!" David shouted toward the band, who responded by spontaneously bursting into the tune of *Dixie*.

October 22nd, 1864

General Vandehoff's gaze was fixed upon the sullen troops who gathered to warm themselves around the multitude of campfires.

Outside in the thick mud, his army had lost the fervent excitement of war as now visions of demise, disease, and hunger haunted their memories and the dissolute fighters from the South contemplated nothing but survival.

Yellow hue from candlelight exposed his weather-beaten and war-drained face. Deep lines of worry now furrowed on his forehead and creased his stubbled cheeks.

Piercing screams of death had long since replaced the music of the polka, and the satisfying warmth of the ball had dimmed and faded into a long distant memory as now torrential cold rain unleashed its endless patter on the general's sodden tent.

He was reflecting on the wanton loss of life. He shuddered, but not because of the cold night air. It was because he could still hear the wailing of pain echoing in his ears and he could see the mass of dead, bloodless faces of his young men.

The past few years had been nothing but hardship, desolation, and cruelty which he could never have imagined. Battles, skirmishes, advances, and retreats had now left deep ingrained scars of disappointment and horror which plagued his every thought.

He opened his battered travel chest and reached down to rummage through his belongings.

His hand ran across the newly delivered knitted socks and vests which he had requested for the approaching winter, and his fingers flicked the bundled edge of the letters from home before finally his hand settled upon his treasured LeMat.

Still, his mind was occupied with the wasted loss of lives, both young and old, and he began to contemplate the fearful sunrise and the human slaughter that was planned for the arrival of the new dawn.

He was disillusioned by the ease with which his men had sacrificed their lives without considering the consequences that were now laden upon young widows, fatherless children, and wrecked parents.

His conscience was heavy with guilt as a result of his decisions and actions. Now he questioned his responsibilities and beliefs as he realised the years of annihilation seemed insignificant to his superiors as they pressed on issuing orders for relentless assaults in Missouri on both the Union army and innocent civilians who were not too long ago considered his fellow countrymen.

He wiped the damp cold barrel of the LeMat with his kerchief. The shine of yesteryear had waned and battle soot had replaced the shimmer. He spun the barrel and inserted fresh ammunition as he had no doubt that early the following day he would once again be using the notorious life-taker.

General Vandehoff organised his assembly as the morning sun's rays bore through the low-hanging dull clouds. The orders issued by his commander, Major General Sterling Price, were simple: a frontal attack on an exposed Union cannon line which was positioned on the banks of the Blue River.

Removal of the artillery would permit Major General Price to advance upon Kansas and continue with his extermination of the Union forces and federal sympathisers in Missouri.

Price's mission was to capture the state for the South, and now only the surrender of Kansas stood in his way.

Vandehoff had received intelligence from Price that the thirty cannons were inadequately defended, but they must be captured or destroyed because they were positioned to prevent the advancement of the Southern army. Leading a cavalry charge, Vandehoff would surprise and overrun the Union defenders before the cannons could be satisfactorily discharged.

Today Vandehoff's rallying speech was to be short. He had delivered many, and now the formality meant nothing to him or his troops other than a few insincere rousing words before being faced with impending butchery.

His eyes were narrow and veined, but it was not due to excessive bourbon; sleep had evaded him.

Not only had the many losses of life plagued him throughout the long night, he was also well aware his troops now lacked food, strength, and ammunition for a fight. They were exhausted, demoralised, and in no condition to engage with the well-stocked army from the North.

"Today I will share your fate and battle for you as you have battled for me. I have a great deal to say, but I will economise, as in a few minutes we will encounter the enemy of the North who intends to invade your lands, destroy your homes, defile your families, and desecrate the graves of the deceased. They will show no mercy or kindness regardless of age, condition, or sex, and they will ensure you have no homes to return to once this war is over."

Each word was loud, clear, and audible to all, but he knew as he drew breath to finish that his appeal was lost on the unresponsive faces which simply yearned for a return home.

"Stand by your convictions, men, and God will stand by you." He waved his arm to signal the bugle call for the attack. "God's grace will be upon you all today!"

Without any further hesitation, General Vandehoff spurred his Arabian and thrust down the green embankment and towards the ford in the Blue River.

Hooves thundered, and the ground shuddered as the heavy cavalry horses threw divots high as, at full speed, they left behind them the shelter and protection of the thick woodlands.

Exposing themselves on the barren field, they all released in unison a fanatic rebel war cry and hurtled with their heads hung low towards the ford.

Ahead in the distance, the general focused upon the half-naked enemy scrambling into positions at the side of their cannons. Faster and faster he urged forward his men and, buoyed by what he had seen, he withdrew his sabre and raised himself in the saddle, waving his sword in the air.

The ensuing chargers yelled and screamed with excited anticipation as they realised they were gaining ground fast without retaliation from the unprepared enemy.

Water splashed high and wide as the horses hit the ford at full speed and momentarily blinded the soldiers at the rear but, within seconds, the Confederates had fractured the ford and were heading up the steep embankment towards the row of cannons.

Suddenly Vandehoff's eyes locked upon branch movements to the right of the cannons and a shudder grasped him as his entire body braced.

An unwanted clasp of fear embraced all his senses, and he had no time to react as grey smoke bellowed out from behind the trees and musket balls hurtled towards him. The sound of the discharge reached his ears at the same time bullets thudded deep and indiscriminately into the moving targets. Piercing horse screams and crimson erupted from all directions as horses dropped and soldiers were blown apart.

Vandehoff was thrown backwards over his horse as a projectile ripped straight through his throat. Confusion, fear, and panic spread as the charge drew to a halt.

The few remaining mounted rebels desperately scoured for leadership as they struggled to hold firm their distressed mounts, but all about them was disarray as dead horses pinned the wounded, screaming men in the mud and disorientated bleeding soldiers staggered aimlessly in the pungent gun-smoked air. All of them had lost all sense of reality and their minds were vacant of all conscious behaviour.

Vandehoff pressed his left hand hard on the burning rupture on his neck, but the flowing blood oozed easily through his fingers.

He staggered upright, gasped for breath, and withdrew the LeMat. Turning to face the reloading Union troops who had stepped out from the woods, he levelled his arm and fired off one poorly aimed shot.

He did not see if his shot had been successful as a trio of lead balls shattered open his head and chest, nor did he hear the call of his name by one of his loyal troopers.

Private Willard Muldoon had seen the general thrust from his horse and he was in the process of rushing to his aid when the second volley of shots exploded.

Dropping onto his knees by the side of the general, Willard Muldoon cupped the back of General Vandehoff's head and scanned quickly for signs of life, but confronted with only the general's death grimace he wasted no more time and sprang back to his feet as behind him he could hear the roar of nearing Union troops who now charged down the embankment with their bayonets cast out in front of them.

Upright and poised ready to flee for his life, Muldoon glimpsed the LeMat which was protruding out of the reddy-coloured mud. Instinctively, he reached down and grasped his fingers around the walnut handle, then without precise aim he discharged all the remaining shots in the direction of the onrushing troops.

With his demise only seconds away, he sprinted as fast as he could towards the ford, but as the rest of the fleeing Confederates scarpered in the same direction from where they had just travelled, Muldoon veered to the left and dropped exhausted into a foliage-covered furrow.

Although uninjured, he gasped hard over and over to fill his fifty-year-old lungs with fresh air. He pressed his body down flat and hard into the boggy depth of the undergrowth, praying he had not been seen, and he clamped his eyelids tight as if to block out the death shrieks of his compatriots as the Union troops massacred the exhausted, the wounded, and the weak who could not escape beyond the ford. Muldoon lay still for longer than he ever imagined he could. Only allowing his chest to rise, he took in deep composing breaths of the chilling Missouri air. His aged body was wracked with cramp pains and his purple skin began to cool as slowly he began to recover from the lung-bursting flight.

The shooting had stopped and so had the pleas and the groans of the wounded and gradual serenity befell across the meadow of death, but still Muldoon dared not move. He had urinated himself for relief, but this did not stop his entire body from stiffening as the long minutes turned into endless hours without him daring to raise his head for fear of capture.

In the far distance, he could hear voices of men and activity. Although he could not be certain, he thought the tones were expressed with a Northern cadence and so he waited until complete darkness had shrouded the meadow before he allowed himself to turn and raise his head to peer out at the surroundings.

Clouds blocked out any emerging stars and the meadow was bereft of any moonlight. It was difficult to see beyond a few yards, but in the distance on the northern side of the slope, he could just make out the orange flare of campfires and lanterns.

He squinted hard across all directions and finally, convincing himself he would not get a better opportunity to make his escape, he quietly raised himself from the crease in the undergrowth and, being careful where he planted his steps, crouched his way in the opposite direction from the illumination until he was deep within the dense blackness of the woodland.

Chapter 2

Oct 25th, 1864

Willard Muldoon wandered slowly through the dense woodlands, open barren fields, and again back into timbered thickets, devoid of any knowledge of where he was heading and all sense of direction. He had carefully walked throughout the night to remain concealed, only resting during the daylight hours.

Now, as the dawning light began to cut through the tall trees and cast its silver sprays of light downwards, he could hear voices in the distance.

He paused as he deliberated his actions, then with caution, he continued on in the dark shadows to move closer towards the source of the disruption which lay deep within the serenity of the forest.

He held perfectly still, only allowing his face to twist into a quizzical frown as in the distance he eyed and scrutinised a small army camp. He remained wary and suspicious of the soldiers' loyalties because all he could see was a variety of different coloured outfits and he could not determine if the soldiers' allegiances were for the South or the North.

Muldoon was well accustomed to seeing the impoverished fighting men of the South clothed in rags and garbed in homespun uniforms of brown, green, and occasionally blue, but he could clearly see that a handful of these soldiers were wearing the uniform of the enemy.

However, he was now groggy, his feet were sore and hunger contracted hard within his empty stomach, and knowing he was near to exhaustion he decided to edge nearer to the camp for a clearer view.

"What ya doing snooting out here in the dark, soldier?" Muldoon stiffened and instinctively raised both his hands above his head as he felt the steel of a barrel press hard into his spine.

"I got spilt from my outfit and I'm lost. That's all."

"Oh yeah? When and where was this, old timer?"

Muldoon recognised the local accent. He assumed his captor was either a Southern soldier who was genuinely suspicious of the stranger or a Northern sympathiser from the Missouri area.

"Few days back. We succumbed to a surprise attack and we had to split in all directions b'cos bullets were howling down on us like a swarm of locusts." He didn't lie.

"Swarm of what-custs? ... Ah never mind. Who ya serving with?" Muldoon noted that the voice seemed particularly boyish.

"The 6th Cavalry..... Missouri. We got damn near hog-walled by some sneaky Union patrol." He slowly turned his head to the side as he spoke to try and glimpse his captor.

"And what direction would this be?"

"Hellfire, friend. I've no idea. I've been walking for near to three days now and I'm at a loss for all directions. All I know is that we were back in a small channel near the Blue River. We were heading onto Westport. That's about all I know." He stumbled slightly, his legs weak and unsteady.

The information was not replied to. Muldoon knew the stranger was contemplating what to do next, so he prompted with an ultimatum.

"As I said, friend. I've been out in these woods three days now and I'm all done, so either take me in or shoot me in the back b'cos I'm well past caring right now and I'm afraid I can't stand up for much longer."

The stranger assessed the short old man for signs of danger. His eyes quickly scanned up from the worn boots to the mud-covered body and then to the grey covering of thin hair on the soldier's head.

"Well, it seems as though you've dropped on mighty lucky this morning, fella."

"Yeah. How so?" Muldoon twisted his neck now as far as he could, but he still could not see the shadowy face to his rear.

"Well, it just so happens that these here folks you've been a-peepin on is the Missouri bushwhackers, and that mighty fine and dandy fella you see over there next to that tent, well that is the one and only William Anderson."

Muldoon felt the iron rod move away from his back and rise slightly over his shoulder until it was pointing in the direction of the tent.

"He's been our chief since we had a little discord with Quantrill."

Muldoon swallowed hard. He had heard hideous firsthand accounts of both Quantrill's and Bloody Bill Anderson's murderous exploits around the muddy waters area of the Midwest.

The young man was oblivious to his prisoner's reverence and he continued. "You'll have to forgive me for being a little titchy because we know a sly Union assembly has been hightailing us for this past week gone."

"Well maybe now you can lower the scuttle pot and show me some of your Southern hospitality." Muldoon slowly stepped sidewards. "I'd be mighty obliged if you can let me rest up a while and fill my belly with some hot coffee and maybe a little food you got going spare?"

He was almost at the point where he could stand no more and so he now fully turned to face the gun holder.

"Whoa! Just steady on there, mister. Don't you be getting all jumpy on me now." The man held firm the rifle and slanted the barrel towards Muldoon's chest. "We'll have to see what Bill says first."

Muldoon squinted twice to clear his eyes in the dull light. He was shocked to see the expression of a youth who was still a few years off reaching the end of his growing years.

"Well, let's get to it, boy, before I die out here on my feet." He slumped to rest his body against a tree.

"Don't call me boy." The young man's eyes widened at the offence. "My name is Clelland Miller. My friends call me Clell." He pronounced it as Kell.

"Mighty pleased to meet you, Clell. I'm Muldoon. Private Willard Muldoon from Taney County, Missouri. Now can we please get to moving before I keel over?" He offered out a weak handshake.

Foliage cracked beneath the feet of the two approaching rebels, arousing caution and suspicion within Anderson's troopers. Drawing their weapons instinctively, silence fell upon the camp until the pair of darkened figures reached a rupture of light between the trees.

"Lower your guns, fellas," Miller shouted. "It's me, Clell, and I'm bringing in a fellow Missourian."

"What's going on, Clell?" asked one of the nearest soldiers with his eyes fixed upon the ragged veteran.

"It's ok, Frank. He is one of our own," Clell replied, motioning with his free hand for the soldiers to lower their weapons.

"Are you sure, Clell?"

"You sure he is not just a shirker?" shouted another soldier across the camp, but Muldoon did not hear Clell's reply nor any other words as unconsciousness enveloped him.

Faces blurred, words became unclear and the roaring fire in front of him glazed into an orb as he relented against the control of his senses and succumbed to blackness, dropping to the floor unconscious.

The smell of hot hickory coffee and pork drifted into Muldoon's nostrils and roused him from the unintentional slumber. He could hear muffled voices as he galvanised himself into a semi-recumbent position.

Although the sun was high above, a campfire still burned fiercely to quell the cold October bite.

With his vision still blurred, he could not focus on the surrounding faces which peered upon him; however, he recognised the tones of young Clell.

"Get this down yer clacker, Willard." Slowly Muldoon's eyes became accustomed to his surroundings, and he realised Clell was holding under his nose a jug of hot coffee.

Now Muldoon could see that seated around the campfire was a collection of rough-faced warriors who were all staring quizzically directly at him.

"Get ya back up on ya feet in no time at all." Clell now hovered the jug nearer to Muldoon's accepting lips. His face crinkled as the hot bitter taste exploded on his tongue and he shook his head as the liquid, which was hot and dark, soured on his taste buds. The cloggy liquid did not resemble coffee, but he willingly took a few more sips until he was alert enough to take the jug from Clell and hold it unassisted.

"Been out a good few hours there, partner," someone from the other side of the fire announced. "We figured you'd be hungry so we've rustled you up some fresh pork hock and cornbread."

"You can thank a kindly farmer over yonder trees." Clell held out a wooden bowl containing the steaming replenishment.

"I'd mercifully welcome that," Muldoon admitted with an ear-to-ear smile as saliva quickly built within his mouth.

"Now don't be givin the old fella too much now," warned another young-looking brute seated opposite. "You don't want to be giving him gut rot seein as he ain't eaten in a while."

"I know that, Jesse. I ain't stupid."

"Just saying, Clell. Food's too precious to puke it all back."

"Think I don't know that, Jesse."

Willard Muldoon just watched. He was too frail to inject himself into the banter, but he became uneasy when another man entered the conversation.

"I'd rather cut his throat and scalp him right now than see our food go to waste." Muldoon's eyes flicked across to the morose-looking menace who spoke as he stoked the fire.

"Arr, you go scoot, Archie. If it's wasted, you can take it out of my rations." Undeterred, Clell slopped more food out of the Dutch oven to replenish Muldoon's bowl.

"Here you go, Willard. This will soon ditch your tummy jitters."

No one noticed the approaching shiny decorative black leather boots that trod their way towards them.

"I see you awake, old timer."

Muldoon twisted to look over his shoulder in the direction of the deep, bellowing voice above.

"Are you with us?" The pitch was not a question, and Muldoon understood its undertone.

"I ain't got anywhere better to be." He replied to the tall and bearded intimidating man who was dressed in all black.

"Is that so?"

"We're all a-fightin for the same side, aren't we?" Muldoon recognised the man as Bloody Bill Anderson. He had encountered many honchos before, and although he was in his senior years and weak, he was able to repost with ease and without getting tongue-tied or showing any sign of intimidation.

Bill held his inflated stance and stared down as he assessed the capabilities of the aged private.

"When you've finished up with the bowl, come over and see me in my tent. I want to pluck your brains." Bill nodded toward the assembly around the fire. "Eat up men, and enjoy your fare because we will be having breakfast in hell tomorrow."

Then he departed as quickly and quietly as he had appeared.

"Never mind Bill. He's just itching to kill a few Yankees, that's all," Clell said.

"That n' Colonel Cox's blue bellies are getting to vex him." Jesse added.

"Nah, they can't be anywhere near us," Clell declared.

"Bill will just want to know if you've come across any of em out there in the woods." Jesse held a self-assured glint, denoting he knew more than everyone else seated around the fire.

"Hold your tongues, you two," Archie interjected. "We ought not to be talking too much in front of Mister Muldoon here until we all get a little more acquainted." His eyes narrowed and fixed directly on the stranger opposite as he spoke.

Muldoon ate and drank the hickory coffee in silence, aware that the eyes of the bushwhackers were upon him.

He sensed Archie's superiority over the group, and it did not surprise him when no more questions were asked and nothing more was divulged. After a few minutes had passed, he thanked Clell for the refreshments and stretched out his stiffened aching limbs and swollen toes before heading towards Bloody Bill's tent.

After a call of introduction from the guard outside the tent, Anderson pulled open the canvas and, with an inviting smile, beckoned Muldoon to enter.

Anderson had removed his dark jacket and Muldoon could not prevent his eyes from glaring at the guerrilla's black overshirt which was highly decorated with elaborate heavy embroidered flowers around the neck, front, and pockets. A thick brown leather belt was pulled tight around his waist which holstered two pistols, a knife, and a heavy-looking purse.

Tucked in the side and rear of the belt were another two pistols. Anderson's raven hair and beard were long and shiny and his face weathered ruddy.

Muldoon did not comment on the amount of armoury on display.

"Would you like a shot?" Anderson asked Muldoon as he poured himself a measure of moonshine.

"Think I'll have to decline, Mister Anderson… thank you." Muldoon half-smiled and tilted his head to indicate his disappointment. "You see, I don't think my insides are good for holding down any of the strong stuff just yet."

"Ah well then. Maybe after our victory tomorrow." Anderson raised the glass as if to offer a toast and Muldoon simply smiled.

"You look to me like…… erm, let's say an experienced soldier, Willard." He downed the moonshine. "It is alright if I call you Willard, isn't it?"

"Sure." Muldoon wanted Anderson to get to the point of the parley.

"Seen plenty of service en' all." Anderson's eyebrows rose, signalling he wanted to hear Muldoon's story.

"Guess so," he obliged. "Served with General Vandehoff since sixty-three and before that, I was with General Albert Sidney Johnston until he met with his maker at Shiloh."

"Shiloh? Ain't too many of our fellas around to tell about the heroics of Shiloh."

"Oh, I ain't boasting. I've seen things in the field of death, Mister Anderson, men just ain't supposed to see." Muldoon closed his eyes and shook his head as if to cast out scarred memories and unsightly apparitions.

"Is that just so?" Anderson did not give Muldoon an opportunity to expand. "I'd like to hear more about Shiloh, but right now I'd be grateful to hear how you found your way here and what you may have observed whilst travelling this way," he paused to empty the contents of the glass into his mouth, then he expanded his lungs and blew out the afterburn vapours before adding, "and particularly what you know about Lieutenant Colonel Samuel P. Cox." Muldoon was invited to sit whilst he narrated the events of the last few days.

Visibly disappointed not to be given any news regarding General Cox's recent movements, Anderson pitched straight into a tirade concerning the enemy.

"Willard. Do you know that just last week Cox's gutless Federals killed six of my men? Scalped them and left them out in a field to rot and be pecked on."

He paused not for Muldoon to comment, but to refill his glass. "I am an honourable man, Willard, and too forthright to permit any of my men to scalp a white man, but from now on I will show the Feds that I will kill their men with as much steel and rapidity as anybody, and from this day forward I ask for no quarter and I give none, for every Union soldier I can put my finger on will die like a dog."

Stopping to empty his glass and then quickly refilling it again, his eyes seemed to flash with a manic vitality and a deep hunger for blood that resembled the glare of the wildest of animals.

"Tomorrow we are going into Albany to replenish our supplies and I've been informed there is a dozen or so Billy Yanks camping in the streets to protect the Northern sympathisers the town's folk have taken to harbouring." He moved up close to Muldoon. "So I'm figuring we should be getting some fun tomorrow." He smiled and winked. "And plenty of it. Are you sure you're still with us, Willard?"

Relieved the examination was over, Muldoon walked across the camp to return to Clell and his comrades. His eyes swept across the relaxed troops as they played the fiddle, dealt cards, snoozed, attended to their weapons, and spread tales of past glories and exaggerated reminiscences.

He was questioned enthusiastically by Clell and the group even before he had squatted to seat himself near the warmth of the fire.

The gang seemed far more at ease now Muldoon had been vetted by Anderson and they soon lost interest in his accounts.

Deciding to ease the boredom by kicking off a game of poker, they moved in closer to circle around a crate and, as they did so, one of the gang members finally decided to introduce himself to Muldoon.

"Archie Clement from Johnson County," said the short young man with a wide leery smile.

To Archie's left, a tall older man tilted forward his head and muttered simply, "Frank." Muldoon acknowledged him with his own nod.

"Ed Miller," said another man, rising to offer out his hand.

"Nice to meet ya," replied Muldoon as their hands clasped to shake.

"Bob Foston," called out a man who tipped his hat.

"Jesse," greeted the last of the young men with a quick nod.

"Dealing ya in, Willard?" asked Clell with puerile eagerness.

"Thanks, Clell, but not right now. I figure I need to rest up a while," Muldoon replied as he hunkered down close by the fire to wiggle himself comfortable.

The gamblers babbled incessantly, immaturely ridiculed and taunted one another as the game faltered and intermittently broke up. They stretched out their legs and gnawed on dry meat, then after a few minutes it all restarted again and they continued to tease and taunt one another over and over with laughter lasting deep into the cold night.

Thoroughly tired and through slitty eyes, Muldoon studied the countenances of the new acquaintances in the dull orange half-light.

All the men were young but, whilst Jesse and Archie looked the same age as Clell, Frank, Bob and Ed seemed about five years older and possibly in their early twenties. These three conducted themselves with a greater controlled maturity than the youngsters.

Archie, Frank and especially Jesse caught Muldoon's attention and intrigued him. Archie was brash, loud and although of a small frame he was weak-looking with a small pale face. However, Muldoon cautiously noted that he exhibited a boldness beyond his youth and a mean self-assuredness.

Both Frank and Jesse were also assured, but their poise was one of a malign calculated calmness. Jesse seemed to have a cold countenance which was enhanced by deep expressionless eyes and a prominent chin dimple which could not go unnoticed.

Frank was of a similar appearance in looks and dress, but he had the beginnings of a dark handlebar moustache and a chin full of whiskers which aged his youthfulness.

Muldoon was later to deduce from the ribbing that Frank and Jesse were brothers, as were Clell and Ed, and that all four of them had grown up together in the same county.

He learned that Clell and Jesse had disobeyed their fathers and after suffering numerous beatings they had skipped out of town to join up with their older kin to fight with Bloody Bill's partisan rangers.

The late-night bragging and bravado continued to the annoyance of Muldoon and, to ignore the gang's immaturity, he laid his hand over his face and clasped both his mouth and eyes shut.

"I can outfight, shoot and outrun any man ten years older than me," he heard Jesse respond to Ed's teasing.

Throughout the duration of the card games and the long cold night, Muldoon listened to suspected fabrications of alcohol-induced boasts and tales of chivalry against the hostiles. The gang's exploits within Bloody Bill's army were drunkenly conversed and recalled. He reluctantly had to listen with nervous disgust at the guerrillas' recollections and their perceptions of bravery which Muldoon recognised as pure butchery, rape and murder.

"When we're all done in Albany, I'm gonna wet my peckerwood into a nice big pussy pie again just like I did in Centralia," he heard Clell slur.

"That's the only way you'll ever get a dip," Frank teased.

"Not true." Clell grinned. "I've got plenty of silver coins." He held out a bag containing his night's winnings, then he added, "Anyways the girl in Centralia enjoyed it."

"Oh yeah? How you figure that out, Clell?" Archie asked.

"Well, she was all wiggling and moaning in my ear. She kept on sayin don't, don't, don't stop and then when I'd finished off she begged me to come back and see her when the war is over." Clell's face beamed a devilish boastful smirk.

"You dumb shit, Clell!" Archie shouted. "She was hollering don't! don't! and stop, stop!" Laughter erupted around the fire.

"And no doubt if you ever do go back to rekindle your acquaintances you can bet all your God damn winnings that her angry-arsed husband will be ready and waiting out back in the shitter to shoot your balls off," Frank added.

"Ah shut it. You're jestin with me b'cause whilst I was busy poking with a woman, you were poking the eyes out of those two blue bellies." Again laughter broke out around the campfire as Archie reached to his belt and produced to hold aloft two scalps.

"Get it right, Clell, poking and scalping….. poking and scalping."

Muldoon remained carefully unmoved by the madness he witnessed, his face hiding the disgust and shame he now felt from being associated with these rebels. He was a traditionalist who believed war should be fought between men in a field well away from innocent townsfolk, and besides he had a wife and family back home and he prayed that should the Union forces breach his home county they would perform their duties with more dignity and respect than the heathens surrounding the campfire in front of him.

He now understood what Anderson had in mind for Albany and he did not have any appetite for the unsavoury violence, knowing Clell and his friends were capable of delivering more fear than fun.

He pulled down the brim of his hat lower to dim the firelight as he tried hard to avoid listening to more of the damning tales and he occupied himself by inspecting Vandehoff's LeMat. He wiped off the blood-dried mud and spun the bullet cylinder, marvelling at the now visible ornate decor.

"Mighty fine piece you got there, old friend," Clell honestly recognised.

"Sure is," Muldoon agreed. "It belonged to General Vandehoff."

"A General?" quizzed Clell.

Willard Muldoon explained how he came to own and care for the gun, then he went into great detail explaining how the gun worked, expressing his knowledge of the finer mechanisms.

"This gun is unique and rare in the fact that it has two barrels. One conventional for distance shooting and one made for firing off buckshot," he let his fingers stroke across the engraving, "both deadly in equal measures. They say in the early years these were designed and issued only to our generals and yes sir, they are quite a find now."

Then he felt the need to obscure the LeMat from the suddenly interested prying eyes around the fire by slipping the pistol under his belt and beneath his mud-covered grey jacket.

The rest of the night could only be described as an uneasy rest.

 Muldoon was not at ease with the company, he did not share their ambitions for the approaching morning and he did not trust them.

After digesting the campfire tales of the gang's perceived warfare he now feared that if he was captured by Union forces whilst he was with Anderson's company he would not find nor receive any of the prisoner-of-war normalities or any sympathetic treatment from his foes because the brutal reputation of Anderson's troops would have spread amongst the Northerners to motivate a speedy extermination.

He considered slipping away in the night, but he considered it too risky knowing the surrounding area was populated with the Union patrols he encountered at Blue River and Cox's troops which were out searching for Anderson and his cronies. Also, he feared that if he failed to safely escape the boundary of the guerrilla camp, Anderson's retribution would be swiftly administered by the noose. Damned by doubt, he decided to stay put for the night and try to rest with his hand gripped tightly around the valuable weapon.

It was Bloody Bill Anderson himself who roused the lethargic rebels by pulling back his canvas vestibule with vigour and eager spirit. He stood tall and erect, dressed in all black with his hat proudly displaying a bright yellow star.

His belt was laden with four pistols and another one in each hand as he looked upwards to the hazy morning sky, bellowing out demoniacal calls for his men to pack up, move out, and unleash hell and havoc upon Albany.

The seven-mile trek through the green wastelands to Albany passed uneventfully. The rebels were buoyant and expectant, but they kept their clamour controllably low to assist in encroaching undetected for as long as possible.

Muldoon had been issued with a horse so that he could journey along with the other two hundred or so bushwhackers.

It was no secret to him the large Morgan had been captured from the enemy, as it was still dressed with a Union saddle and carbine boot.

Bloody Bill Anderson halted the Confederate line on the edge of the woodlands so that he could observe the wooden adobe straggle of buildings which made up Albany in the distance.

Jesse, Archie and Frank were displaying reckless eagerness to attack and spill blood, but the rest of the gang flanking Muldoon seemed apprehensive and edgy.

Muldoon had experienced the battle quivers many times before and he flexed his muscles and held his breath longer than he normally would to calm his tension and clear his thoughts.

With no suspicious activities being noted, Anderson calmly led his troopers out of the shadows of seclusion and onto the vast open wasteland, continuing the calm approach towards the sleepy small town.

After travelling about five hundred yards on the undulating grassy terrain, Anderson increased the tempo of the approach, then after cantering for five hundred yards, he raised his hand and yelled.

"Here we go, boys. Let's give em hell." He then heeled his mount into a gallop and urged his rebels to follow suit.

Releasing their own intimidating screams and ear-piercing wails of attack, the rebels drew their weapons and charged fiercely towards the stillness of Albany.

Unable to control their excitement any longer, a couple of premature shots were discharged into the low-hanging clouds and within an instant the entire throng was replicating the death-chilling shots. Thick discharge smoke shrouded the band of executioners as they frenziedly charged their way at pace to within two hundred yards of the first building.

Muldoon was ringed in tight amongst the pack and unable to see much beyond dust, gun smoke and the rear ends of galloping horses. He had no alternative but to hold on tight to the reins, keep his head down low and keep pace with the pack.

The powder stung his eyes, but the water did not prevent him from noticing Anderson's sinister smile as, in the fast-approaching distance, the townsfolk could be seen scarpering for shelter and a few blue-clad men began to throw together a makeshift barrier.

A couple more Union soldiers could be seen beginning to prep and aim their rifles in a strangely calm manner, but this did not concern Anderson nor his troops.

A few shots sounded and puffs of smoke were seen but no one was felled as the charge continued almost unopposed until suddenly movement in the branches to the right caught Muldoon's eye but it was too late to respond and an unexpected discharge of rifles was heard.

Muldoon held the squint over his right shoulder as bullets thudded purposely into both man and beast. He could just see through the bulk of the rebels a blue wave of Union cavalry approaching fast from the woodlands. Some rebels became aware of the surprise attack and veered their horses off towards the right, but as they began to arc, another blast of weaponry sounded off to their left side.

"It's a trap boys! Somebody's squealed on us!" Anderson raged. Confusion began to spread as the chargers pulled to an unplanned stop. The rebels frantically twisted their heads and flicked their panicked eyes in all directions, but there was no obvious escape route without direct confrontation from a superior-sized enemy advance.

Some of the men turned their horses to the rear, but advancing out of the thick undergrowth behind them more blue uniforms could be seen levelling their rifles.

Chaos ensued as lead reigned its full destruction into the tight pack.

Blood sprayed high, screams from both man and beast were expelled as this time bodies were blasted out of saddles and horses began to uncontrollably flee as bolts of pain pierced deep into their hides.

As with everyone else, Muldoon struggled to control his horse and in the melee he found himself close to Anderson. He saw Clell and his cohorts fleeing towards the aimed rifles at the edge of the forest but as he heeled the Morgan to join them, Anderson and a few men close by him began to charge towards the town and his motion was lost as his terror-stricken horse followed Anderson's pack.

"Let's at em boys. Send em all to Hell!" hollered out Anderson as he charged onwards, dropping the reins to fire off his pistols with both hands.

By now a substantial enemy force had formed a line at the edge of the town, but this did not deter Bloody Bill Anderson from continuing with his ill-fated frontal attack.

Muldoon could see a manic glee had filled Anderson's eyes and a devilish energy seemed to blast through him.

He was inhumanly alert and his face radiated an expression of invincibility and a glint of eternal life.

Muldoon tried hard to suppress his Morgan's charge, but the horse grew more frenzied as whistling missiles, shrieks and yells swarmed around them until moments later it too was felled by another discharge of lead.

Muldoon was tossed high and clear of the dead bulk, but he hit the ground hard and rolled and bounced uncontrollably until his momentum was stopped by another dead horse. He felt his shoulder snap immediately and seconds later his right ankle began to flap loosely.

Disorientated, without breath and through blurred spinning vision he could just make out Anderson laying in front of him with blood oozing out from the middle of his forehead. Eyes wide open but fixed skywards, the look of invincibility had vanished and death had settled upon his lifeless body. Muldoon's mouth began to fill with hot blood and his attentions were overwhelmed by spasms of riveting pain in his ankle, shoulder and midriff.

He placed the flat of his hand on the burning sensation in his stomach and it became flooded with hot claret. He spat out a mouthful of bile into the thick smog as pain surged and ravaged through him, but he could do nothing to repress it. Blood pulsed quickly from the wound and expanded across the grey of his coat as the red saturation spread.

Now the brightness of the mid-morning light began to fade into dullness, and the surrounding combinations of death wails and bullets began to diminish into a muddled low hum which reminded him of rustling trees.

He did not see the blue uniform of Lieutenant Potter Brompton approach and stand over his motionless body to stare into his ashen face as seconds earlier he had readily accepted the peaceful and pain-free blackness which had crept upon his soul as he expelled his final breath.

Brompton nudged the lifeless corpse of Willard Muldoon with his foot, and the dead man released an uncontrollable grunt.

Blood dripped out of the side of his mouth as the remnants of his final breath forcibly expelled from his lungs and his limp hand slid from the hole in his body to drop into the blood-stained soil by his side.

At that moment Brompton's eyes cast upon and locked onto the LeMat which was still tucked in the dead soldier's leather belt.

Chapter 3

June 18th 1866

Potter Brompton sat on the schooner seat, his chin held high and his head straight back. His thoughts were gathered deep inside and he wasn't willing to share them with his wife, Rayne, for fear of upset.

He scanned across the prairie, where the endless green and brown grass extended out in all directions over the enormous landscape. His mind was a conjecture, riddled with thoughts of the war and death, dying, and the wounded. His mind had been forever scarred by the sounds and visions of merciless bloody slaughter. The last four years had left a haunting and recurring scar deep within his subconsciousness and, in peaceful moments like this, he could not prevent the ghosts of the butchery from returning. He gave little thought now to the pre-war years. That chapter in his life was firmly closed, and there was no option for a return.

Nestor Charles Brompton was a proud tobacco plantation owner and prominent politician in Petersburg, Virginia, and he was an ardent secessionist who vehemently opposed his son Potter's association with the Union, and a family crisis ignited when Potter enlisted to fight for the North.

Potter was disowned by his father, Nestor.

He was cut from all funding, the family will, and all inheritance, but now his father's estates, business, and fortunes were all in ruin with the collapse of the Southern economy and the victory of the Union.

Potter had despised his father for his convictions, beliefs, and the treatment he imposed upon his new wife, Rayne, whilst he was fighting amidst the conflict. Nestor did not support Rayne in the absence of her husband and, in an act of defiance aimed to hurt and embarrass his son, Nestor evicted Rayne from the family mansion and ceased all financial support.

Any bond, love, or affection he had for his father was at that point banished, and Potter had developed an indomitable will to prosper without the need of his father's backing.

Due to the uncertainty and unreliability of the meagre army pay, Rayne had to survive by finding work in the local textile mill and from the charity of her own family and friends. She was ejected from all high society privileges, and she lived alone as an unaccepted pauper.

During the many sleepless nights throughout the duration of the war, Potter had planned out his future years. He had no intention of returning home.

He had decided to cut all ties with his Southern-sympathising family and emigrate west to build a new business from the opportunities offered by the expanding western territories.

He looked up high into the clear blue, where he could see hawks soaring above and scouring for food.

His mouth was dry and his stomach began to ache with hunger pains, but he was momentarily distracted as the welcoming sun warmed his face and hands. He pulled the reins to encourage the oxen to continue their pull with momentum. They blew out breath and snorted in recognition of the sound of the harness jangling. It was almost time to shelter, and far away in the distance he noticed a large spread of elm, which indicated a stream or river was nearby. He scanned the horizon again, this time for signs of movement, a shimmer or a cloud of dust in the distance, but there was nothing, as all signs of human habitation had disappeared entirely a few weeks earlier.

Occasionally, over the passing months, the Bromptons had stumbled upon desolate and abandoned small settlements that had been built long ago by hardy pioneers. Built with logs, many were still partially tented, and the sod roof had offered an attractive alternative to stretching out from the cramped feather mattress, which had to be placed on top of stacked boxes and crates belonging to the two travellers.

Potter's face displayed disappointment; he hoped to land upon such an adobe as they trekked towards Denver. His body ached from being seated too long. He longed to stretch out. An old shrapnel wound combined with his disfigured feet constantly reminded him of the twenty battles and six thousand miles he had marched whilst serving for the Union.

He didn't complain. Over the past years he had become accustomed to sleeping outdoors and in rough conditions, but now he yearned for a night under the cover of a solid building, safe from the crying coyotes which had prevented Rayne from sleeping for well over the last week.

Again, he tugged on the reins. His oxen and sturdy wagon had so far served him well, and he was satisfied with his purchases for the expedition. His mind flashed back to the small town of Hannibal, where he resided after the war ended. Re-enlisting for another twelve months, Potter stayed in Missouri to assist with the reconstruction of the state, but he immediately arranged transportation for Rayne to join him as he began to meticulously plan, purchase, and assemble all the equipment, materials, commodities, and supplies he required for the six-month journey across the wilderness and its unknown dangers.

After acquiring diverse and qualitative advice from returning settlers, he had decided to purchase three yokes and six strong oxen to pull his large emigration schooner, with the addition of a cow for fresh milk and cheese. He arranged for a purpose-built staunch canvas cover to be fitted, which was watertight and durable enough to defy the ravages of the winds and storms.

Rayne Brompton feared the perils of the journey after hearing many tales of disaster in the half-savage country, but she busied herself by assembling all the necessities, which included lotions, medical herbs, dried meats, fruit, and some additional luxuries which were to be used as trade or currency in times of emergency.

Potter's other purchases included shovels, ropes, grease, hatchets, a spare wheel, and plenty of ammunition for his rifle and his prized LeMat.

The four months of preparation soon passed for the busy Bromptons, and even though they were together as man and wife, Potter decided it wise to avoid all temptations of lust and abstain from any bedtime activities with his wife for fear of a pregnancy adding more complexity and difficulties to the expected arduous journey. Another mouth to feed and a weak wife was a burden he did not want to risk.

Rayne did not object to the abstinence or the journey Potter had decided to embark upon. She saw it as her duty to abide by her husband at all times and support his decisions without question.

They departed from Hannibal, Missouri, in April along with another nineteen wagons, fifty-five men, ten women, and twenty children; however, it was not long before frustration and dissent began to fester and hinder the progress as regular disagreements regarding the route, speed, and the number of stops erupted from the hotheads who thought they knew a better way of doing everything.

Every evening the travelling men would form a council, pipes would be smoked, and violins would play to laughter and dance, but almost on all occasions, after too much whisky had been swilled down dusty throats, mouths began to shoot off advice and arguments ensued, which often finished with brawls, blood, and tears.

As illness began to spread through the train, Potter decided to split from the main group and continue west unaided. He was not a man short of confidence, and he trusted entirely in his own judgement and abilities. Just north of Kansas, as the main group decided to arch northwards to cross the Big Blue River at a ford, Potter took a route southwards where he knew he could cross the Big Blue by ferry.

The Bromptons had not seen or heard anything from the group of emigrants since that day over one month ago.

Now Potter pulled his schooner to a standstill near a line of trees, and both he and Rayne dismounted at the same time to stretch out their stiffened limbs and assess the stream in front of him.

He had learned the hard way to ensure that if he came across a river or stream, he crossed it before nightfall due to the regular night storms which would frequently swell the stream and overflow its banks with raging torrents, but on this occasion, after he tested the depth by throwing stones and, looking forward to nightfall, he decided to pack up and rest.

He'd had enough of the irksome monotony of being shaken and rocked on the forlorn prairie for one day. The jolting, rocking of the wagon had become torture, and a good rest was needed, along with the simple joy and pleasure he found from watching and attending to the campfire's cheerful blaze.

As was their routine, he would attend to the grazing of the cattle whilst Rayne would collect rocks to form a circle and build up a large fire. She would cook the evening meal and they would eat until the darkness set in and became so complete that they could have been unknowingly surrounded by unidentified demons. At this point every night, they would take cover and wrap up for bed.

As the sun's rays gave way to those of the campfire, the huge flames threw comfort onto their faces every night. The conversation was sparse between the Bromptons as they devoured with relish the nightly ritual of salted pork and beans in almost silence. Occasionally, when time permitted, Rayne cooked bread, dried apples, and steamed fruit loaves, but this was all too rare an occurrence. Often, without her husband's knowledge, she had released unbidden tears of anxiety, and in spite of her stern resolve, the realisation of the sacrifices she was to endure grew within her.

Long gone were the luxuries and comforts of the civil life she had become accustomed to in Hannibal. All had now been replaced with toil, drudgery, and solitary camp work. She had to endure exposure to the daily changing elements, the glare of the midday scorching sun, and the hard dusty winds, which often turned into torrential rainfall and thunderstorms, all of which now began to weaken her without any cessation.

Potter tried to comfort Rayne from a distance and without affection. He was determined not to test his vow of celibacy, but he remained positive and assured Rayne that the promise of a family and prosperity lay in the land of golden promise just beyond the now visible Rocky Mountains.

Earlier that afternoon, once the camp had been set, Potter decided to walk back a few miles to a water basin he had seen amongst dense undergrowth. It was an abundant hunting ground where geese, herons, and badgers congregated. Potter believed the easy prey would be a welcome alternative to the jerky and squirrels which had begun to irritate his stomach.

Hidden and kneeling in the foliage, he began to prep his rifle, but then, almost as a challenge to himself, he laid the rifle flat and withdrew the LeMat. With an assured glint in his narrowed aim, he fired off a volley of four shots at the resting gaggle, and before dark he was greeting Rayne with two large geese draped over his shoulder.

A huge grin crossed his face, but it was not because he was pleased with the success of the hunt. He was excited by the power and the accuracy of the prized pistol, his LeMat, Lieutenant Potter Brompton's LeMat.

The blue night soon faded into black and the sky glistened with the millions of small stars which occupied every view.

Coyotes howled and cried in the echoing distance, and the fear of the menacing night beasts in this sheer loneliness signalled it was time to retire inside the schooner and lie tight with Rayne and the LeMat for company until first light.

This night they spent alone, but it wasn't always the case.

Several times they had been nuisanced by hungry Indians, but Potter had planned for such awkwardness and had packed extra provisions to appease the visitors. By the fourth of these visits, Rayne had become accustomed to the redskins' quiet, taciturn ways. Often they would appear out of the darkness and surround the fire to warm their hands.

Saying very little, they waited for warm drinks and food to be offered, and once consumed and satisfied, they moved on without causing any further distress. Occasionally Potter had traded eastern items for fresh meat and fish, and on one encounter with a friendly Arapaho, he swapped a small bag of sugar for an entire deer's leg, which was a welcome relief from the dry salted pork.

At daybreak, Rayne cooked corn cakes and bacon while Potter packed up the camp and prepared the oxen and the cow. They crossed the stream with ease and travelled across the changing landscape without delay. With the exception of the stirring wind and a couple of streams, there was no noise and no reason for concern.

The sun began to rise higher in the cloudless sky and Potter could see the distant gentle undulations beginning to change into timber-covered mountains.

His eyes followed the dusty byway which was packed down into hard wheel ruts where the iron of untold numbers of prairie schooners, livestock, and horses had passed before them. He could see without any obstruction as the trail diminished into a faint line far away.

They continued on slowly until the afternoon sun began to fade and Potter noticed a small rising dust cloud on the track ahead. He frowned and narrowed his eyes to focus on the disturbance ahead and yelled to Rayne, who was walking ahead of the wagon, to return and be seated next to him. He was not unduly concerned, as he expected to eventually cross paths with fellow travellers, hunters, trappers, salesmen, and Indians, but he thought it wise to conceal the beauty of his wife and protect her by his side.

Before she had climbed aboard, he had carefully positioned his rifle at his feet and tucked the fully loaded LeMat in his waist belt. His slight tension was soon eased as, travelling in the opposite direction, the source of the dust was confirmed as another schooner.

Drawing to a near halt as the wagons began to manoeuvre past each other on the narrow and deeply rutted track, the Bromptons cast a careful but friendly glance towards the approaching family sat on the front board of the schooner.

"Howdy pard," shouted the eldest male across. "Where ya headin' from?"

Potter tipped his hat and replied, "Headed out of Hannibal ten weeks past." His glare was fixed upon the grey and raccoon Confederate kepi which was set at an angle on the stranger's head.

"Mind if we shake up alongside you and stay the night?" the stranger asked through his toothless mouth.

"Well, it's a little early to call it for the day," Potter replied, but Rayne nudged him in the ribs with the back of her tightened hand. She had scanned the family, and she did not perceive them as a threat, though she was concerned by their weakened appearance.

She pitied them and, with an accompanying slight nod, her eyes opened wider to indicate to Potter that she was eager to have company for the night.

"We really need some friendly company, and besides, I've got something to tell you that you folks need to give serious consideration to," said the stranger, but Potter's eyes were still locked upon the kepi and he did not reply. He knew the gold-braided bugle indicated the traveller had served in the rebel infantry, and he considered uniform wearers of the defeated army dissenters who should be hung and their families banished.

Rayne nudged Potter again, only this time with her elbow and with more force.

"I suppose a couple of hours short won't make any difference, and I guess the family here," he replied, removing his glare to look down at the oxen, "will be glad of a good rest."

"Well thank ya kindly indeed, sir. Mighty gracious of ya." The whole family, who were wrapped together in a large blanket, smiled, revealing relief in unison. Their faces were pallid and gaunt; they displayed the harrowing demeanour of suffering and exhaustion.

"My name is Brody Locke," he swung his hand out to his right, "this is my wife Mattie, her sister Bly, our two boys Forest and Henry, and the new bairn is Mayson."

Potter returned the smile, but he noticed Bly did not raise her white solemn face from its lowered, transfixed position and her eyes remained downwards towards her feet.

"Potter Brompton and my good lady Rayne," he boasted.

"Pleased to make your acquaintance, sir, ma'am," Brody acknowledged, adding, "We'll just hanker down right over here." He pointed two brown-stained fingers towards a flat about twenty yards from the track.

"Alright then. I'll see you when you've got all set," replied Potter, and then in concert both the men yelled out "giddy up" as they exhorted their animals into action.

"I reckon they're snuff dippers from Tennessee," Potter whispered.

"I saw you scowling at his cap," Rayne said, concerned.

"Don't worry. The past is the past," he finished as he pulled to a stop near the shade of a grove of evergreens.

Within the hour, both camps were set and the animals were released to graze. Potter flicked his eyes across the plain to confirm his immediate assumptions that the Bromptons had nothing to fear. It became obvious to Potter as the Lockes made camp that they were very short on provisions.

He could see now the blanket had been removed that all six of them were almost half naked and dressed in rags, which only just covered their skeletal frames.

One of the boys had a large cut across his cheek and his right hand was swathed tightly with a bloodstained cloth. With nothing to cook and no means by which to light a fire, they soon made their way across the twenty yards of dry brown grass.

"As you have probably established by now, Mister Brompton, we've run across some hard times and we are mighty grateful to the Lord for putting us on the same path as you kindly Christians," said the approaching Brody with his eyes fixed upon the flames and the cooking pot.

"Well, you all just come on over and sit yourselves down here," Potter offered, knowing full well that Brody and his following brood were already well in the process of nearing the fire. Rayne ushered the family around the warmth. They did not try to hide their pleasure as the corn soup wafted into their nostrils.

"Been a while, eh?" Potter asked, referring to the last time they had eaten.

"Too long, far too long." Only Brody looked at Potter; everyone else's attention was fixated on Rayne as she poured out the soup into tin bowls.

"Well, I'm sorry we ain't cooked up a little more. We didn't exactly prepare for company," Rayne confessed.

"We got time if you want to throw a little more in the pot," Brody urged.

"Is that so." Potter's reply was not a question, and he did not anticipate a reply because the Lockes were all ravaging the soup like savages, spooning down mouthful after mouthful of the thick stock without raising their heads or pausing for one moment.

After a couple of refills and numerous mugs of coffee, the whole family seemed less agitated and more at ease in the presence of their fellow country kin.

"Where ya heading?" It was Brody who initiated the small talk.

"All the way through to Salinas. I've bought into a merchant's business which, come this fall, will provide supplies for the US Army," Potter stated proudly.

Brody grunted something inaudible, his eyes slanting toward Mattie and Bly, then he raised his head to speak. "Well, I'm sorry to say I have got some terrible news which I must convey to you, Mister Brompton."

"Yeah." Potter decided to ensure the encounter remained formal. Although he had stated to Rayne that he held no grudges against the soldiers of the South, he did not respect the man who seemed to provocatively boast his allegiances by wearing the colours of the rebels long after the war had ended.

"Maybe you'd like to mosey on over to my wagon so we don't alarm Missy Brompton?"

"No, I'm fine right here." Potter remained unmoved and he drew breath to puff out his chest. "Anything which needs to be said can be said right here and out in the open." He placed his left hand trustfully upon his wife's shoulder and his right fingers carefully onto the handle of the LeMat.

"I advise you, Mister Brompton, I really think this is not for Missy Brompton's ears." The Lockes' eyes flicked across to each other again, but they remained silently occupied with their tongues wiping out the near-empty bowls.

"Whilst I have apathy for you and your family's position, Mister Locke, and I'm willing to listen, may I remind you, sir, that you are not qualified to advise me of anything."

It appeared an impasse was about to develop when suddenly one of the boys rolled over onto his side. With his face twisting, he squirmed with pain and began to rub the flat of his palms hard against his griping stomach, which had contorted and tightened as a reaction to him receiving some long-overdue food.

The momentary diversion broke the tension and, as Mattie reassured her son and Rayne started to make a hot compress to relieve the pain, the atmosphere eased.

Once the commotion had calmed, Brody submitted a brief nod to express his gratitude and that now he was ready to begin. He helped himself to more coffee and explained that the family had been journeying out to Boise, Idaho, from Obion County, Tennessee.

"Eighteen wagons in total, all making good progress without incident, when up near Grizzly Pass we encountered a couple of redskins. They approached us with firm but friendly advances. Pretty much the same as all the other redskins we'd come across, but then they got to pressing us more for food n'like and they began to pester us by going into and turning over a couple of the wagon supplies." Brody slid back the kepi and scratched his greasy forehead. "Anyways, we decided to run 'em out of camp, but a few hours later, when we had travelled deep into yonder forest and most of us were sleeping, they snooped in close and attacked us with a devilment I've never encountered before."

Mattie and Bly began to sob, and they hugged each other for compassion, trying hard to ease the painful memories.

"The God damn savages were firing off rifles and arrows in every direction and they were intent on butchering all of us."

Now the boys began to cry and Rayne lowered down to their level, wrapping her arms tight around both their shoulders.

Brody wet his lips on the coffee again, then continued. "As it happens, the men managed to get to their firearms and retaliate just enough to send 'em off scarpering into the woods, but the damage was done and the losses were painful." Brody paused and laid his hand on the shoulder of his sister-in-law, Bly.

"Eight men, three women, and two youngsters were hacked to death without mercy, and poor Bly here, well she's been left a widow at only twenty-one."

Potter glanced a look of condolence towards Bly.

"Sorry for your loss, ma'am," he said, then, closing his eyes briefly, he added, "This is unimaginable."

"What?" Brody asked in an almost challenging way. "What ya implying?"

"It's strange. The natives along these parts are notably cordial and the friendly type." Potter's face bore a quizzical frown.

"Well these redskins ain't cordial and they sure ain't the friendly type. They plain and simply took to plundering and murdering," spat Brody.

Potter was still musing about what Brody had said. "The Arapaho in these parts don't attack white folk." He rubbed his stubbled chin. "It's unheard of, especially without provocation."

Brody moved his face near to Potter and snarled. "Well, you really are as green as they come, ain't you Mister Brompton, because the God damn savages sure attacked us and took to killing women, young 'uns, and bairns real easy and without provocation nor mercy."

"After food? Did they ask for or say anything?" Potter suggested.

"When the first two came, they asked for food to start with and we gave them a little, but they kept on wanting more and soon they became hostile, demanding our guns and ammunition. One of the fellas was from Wisconsin and he was acquainted with their tongue, so we knew what they were after."

Potter shook his head. He suspected these attackers were not natives.

"Eventually we told them to go skoot, and that's when they became aggressive and started rummaging. Our tolerance was broken when they grabbed one of the Hawlings girls and tried to drag her off into the woods."

Brody paused to lubricate his still dry throat with more coffee. "Some of the men retaliated and forced the redskins to leave by kicking their arses out of camp… and I mean literally kicking them out of camp."

Brody cut in and, raising his voice, he persisted. "I've never heard of an attack on this route." Potter was dismayed. "With the treaty and all."

"Just because you ain't heard of any attacks, it doesn't mean they ain't happening. I'm telling you, Mister Brompton, it is dangerous out there on that road ahead." He paused for another slurp of coffee and continued.

"After the attack, we packed up and rode out without delay, but all the next day the God damn red devils kept on firing down on us from within the thick shrubbery, and then throughout the night they kept on raiding us, stealing whatever they could get their ravaging hands on."

He finished off the coffee and shook the mug in the air to blow away any remnants. "At one point they almost got to dragging Mattie away with them. That's when I knew I'd had enough. The entire group was hollering and petrified. All they could do was panic and, there not being many fighting men amongst them, the murderers soon got most of the food and stole the horses. With the vermin after taking our women for their own purposes, I told the group I'd had enough, and I was getting the hell out of the uncertain woods. At the next split in the trek, I headed about to seek a different route home."

Rayne offered a refill of coffee which he eagerly accepted.

"We escaped with nothing more than our lives and we've been surviving, if you can call it that, off the charity of the land ever since."

Brody's eyes had been studying the crates, flour sacks, and especially the hung dried pork. "We'd be duly beholden to you if you can call upon your conscience and pack us up some food to put us on for a few weeks."

Brody's eyes widened and he smiled, but with the silence and hesitation, he sensed Potter's reluctance to oblige his request.

"I've got money in the bank and I can mail you payment to cover my debts for your kindness," he guaranteed.

"It ain't that." Potter shrugged. "You see, we've been aiding the natives already and we're getting kind of low ourselves."

"You must have some scraps you can spare." Wide eyes flickered over the supplies.

"I'm sorry, but I just ain't got nothing to offer you folks," he lied.

He had packed up plenty of extra supplements, including powdered and dry food, but he knew to complete the long trek ahead he would need the additional supplies to use as trade and barter in times of necessity. "We're going to need everything we've got to get through."

"You continuing on?" Brody assumed the Bromptons would put their journey on hold and return east with them until safer times were confirmed.

"Come this far."

"Don't you fear getting attacked?"
All eyes were now examining Potter's face nervously, waiting for his next words.

"We're continuing on," he confirmed without showing any concern.

"I was kind of hoping to persuade you folks to turn back and travel along with us. You must be more than a mite crazy to carry on after what I've told you."

Potter remained silent, and Rayne knew her husband would not alter his decision. He was an expert in managing confrontations, and she knew he would not be for turning.

"It's not too late to change your mind, Mister Brompton." Brody also sensed Potter would not be willing to change his view, and he was dumbfounded.

"My mind is not for changing. First light, we are continuing west."

For the first time, Mattie spoke. "Mister Brompton, are you willing to risk everything you consider precious by heading on towards that pine forest? And put yourselves in terrible peril."

Potter's face flushed. He was not accustomed to being denounced by a female.

"I know how to handle the hostiles. I fear them not. Now Mister Locke, please control your woman and do not let her address me again."

Silence fell around the camp and Brody pressed his lips together tight as he contemplated choosing his response.

He was offended by Potter's denigration, but he knew his family were desperate for more food and he was far too weak to challenge Potter in any form.

"Maybe you can give it a little more consideration while you're resting up tonight," he urged.

"As I said, my mind is made."

Brody relinquished. "Well okay then, Mister Brompton. I'm really sorry to ask again, but what about loaning us some of your supplies you've got stacked up high over there?"

"Again, Mister Locke, as I have already reiterated, I have given all I could spare, including scraps and bones to the Indians and a couple of other fellow travellers who were also in need."

"Mister Brompton. We are desperate and I am pleading to your heart, sir." He clasped his hands as if he was about to say a prayer, but he saw Potter was unresponsive. "I've said I can forward you the money in return for your mercy, or we could trade you that silver daisy chain my wife's got hanging round her neck there."

"Brody!" Mattie called out. "You know this is all I've got left of my mama's."

"No good decorating a corpse, is it, Mattie?" Brody quickly replied.

"You can eat all that's cooked up and keep the chain." Potter offered, pointing to the large bowl hanging over the fire.

"That's accommodating of you, sir, but we need a little something to take on the road with us, and if the chain doesn't take to your liking, how about you prefer something a little more comforting." Brody's eyes opened wider and, holding his hand out in the direction of Mattie, he smiled. "Like say, humping my wife for a while, or maybe you'd prefer to put your dipper in her sis." He moved his hand a little in the direction of Bly. "Or golly, why not do 'em both together."

Mattie's eyebrows raised as a result of her artificial smile.

"Hellfire, they're both real pleasant down there below them pantlets… I can vow for that." Brody's mouth released a perverse, slanted grin. "Surely these two darlings take to your liking."

His offer was met with silence and so, in despair, he felt the need to continue to entice and endorse. "They're both hotter than a pepper sprout in the sack."

Rayne remained unmoved; her face did not reveal her disgust. Both Mattie and Bly's pale and forlorn faces released a tragic, relenting expression, which acknowledged they were also willing to do anything to end their suffering and ensure their survival.

It had been a long time since Potter had felt the tenderness of women, and whilst he found both of the women mildly attractive he was disgusted by the man's desperation and he decided to decline the temptation. He feared once he had broken from abstinence, he would yield and submit regularly to the yearnings of the vice.

"I'm sorry Mister Locke, but I'm afraid I'm going to have to decline your offer." Potter confirmed Brody's fear.

"What? Why in heaven's sake?" All the Lockes sighed with dejected astonishment.

"Afraid so. It ain't that the girls aren't pretty enough, but I must decline because I love my wife and I will not breach her trust nor pain her feelings."

"Why Missy Brompton, you don't object none, do you? You'd like Mister Potter to have a little distraction time, wouldn't you?" Brody was beyond sensing he had insulted the Bromptons, and he appealed to Rayne for her approval and blessing. She turned away from his begrimed face, her expression giving in to a scowl of revulsion.

"Mister Locke! Do not petition my wife." Potter stood tall and positioned himself between Brody and his still-seated wife. "I've told you repeatedly we have nothing to offer."

"God darn you, sir. I've tried to be nice and friendly, so—" Brody was now bereft of all hope. "And I can see that it ain't appealed to your generosity," his face twisted to reveal bitterness, "even though, as you can see, we're near half starved to death and desperate. You're leaving me no choice, Mister Brompton. I'm just gonna have to help myself to some of them supplies over there."

Brody's head nodded slightly to his side to affirm his intentions, and he stepped away from the fire.

Potter matched Brody's stride and stood before him to block him from moving nearer to the supplies.

"I advise you, Mister Locke, not to move one more step any closer to my necessities!"

"I'm sorry sir, but we need it more than you and it looks to me as if you've got plenty to spare some." Potter noticed Brody's shaky hand moving towards his belt knife.

"Get your hands up!" Within an instant, Potter had raised and rested the tip of the LeMat on the chest of the Tennessean. "I will not be threatened, and I warn you, Mister Locke, I will not hesitate to end your life right here and now."

"Might as well shoot me down dead, Mister Brompton." Brody raised his hands high, but he continued to put his foot slowly forward, continuing his approach towards the provisions.

"I'm gonna die anyway. Might as well die nice and quick. Just go ahead. Shoot us all and end our misery right now."

Potter matched the step backward, ordering, "I'm warning you, Mister Locke, one last time. Do not move." He then muttered, "No good son of a bitch."

Brody did not relent, and he forced another step against the barrel of the pistol.

Being a veteran on the killing fields, Potter was experienced enough to see in a man's eyes if he was a natural killer or not and knew Brody was no such killer, but he also knew he was far beyond all rationale and his thoughts and actions were due to his starvation and his family's desperation. But he too felt he had to defend his position due to the uncertainties the Bromptons were sure to face in the long journey ahead.

He knew he had to act with swift directness to halt Brody and stop him from raiding the supplies, so before another step was completed he swung back the LeMat and cracked it hard against Brody's temple, dropping the scavenger limp to the mud.

Everyone remained rigid, with their eyes locked wide upon the two men, and with trepidation they held their breaths to see what happened next.

Potter stood erect over the injured man, raising his arm again in preparation to deliver another blow, whilst at his feet Brody squinted and tried hard to regain his focus. His equilibrium was scrambled, but with panting despair he pulled his face from the dirt and scrambled onto his knees in an attempt to continue towards the supplies.

Rayne screamed out as the loud crack of steel against bone was heard across the camp but the Lockes all still remained unmoved, their motionless and expressionless faces lit by the glow of the flames. They were exhausted of all forms of energy.

The second blow left Brody incapacitated. His white eyes were half shut and blood was spurting from a concave wound in the back of his head. Potter looked down to see if the man was still breathing, and whilst he was still assessing the damage, Rayne had launched herself to be at his side.

Fearing that her husband was not yet finished, she locked her arms around him and begged him to stop the beating.

He seemed oblivious to her frantic plea and shrugged her away with ease. Then he grabbed Brody by his shirt and dragged him unchallenged across the prairie grass to near his wagon, where he released the limp body with one final threat.

"Come anywhere near us again and I'll shoot you dead without delay!"

Then, marching back towards camp, he shouted just what Rayne was expecting. "Pack up. We're moving out."

Potter did not fear the Tennessean, but he feared his desperateness would lead him to be reckless with his life and this would test his resolve to the full and, not wanting to kill a fellow citizen and family man, he decided it wise and to everyone's benefit if he moved out now whilst Locke was crippled and senseless.

He poured out the remaining coffee over the flames of the campfire and stamped down hard on the charred wood and embers with the sole of his boot then, without making any eye contact to avoid arousing any pity or sympathy, he ushered the Lockes out of his camp.

Rayne did manage to scramble together a muslin bag containing a few measly offerings of beans, bones, and some provisions they had saved to offer to the Indian nuisances, but within minutes the Bromptons had left the Lockes alone on the prairie with their faces mantling tragic expressions of numbness and resignation, now knowing they were bereft of all hope.

Potter pulled his wagon to a halt just a couple of miles down the track from the Lockes' camp at the edge of a row of large pines.

He could see through his binoculars the boys were trying to rekindle the Bromptons' fire while Mattie was tending to her inanimate husband, and so he was satisfied they would not be disturbed again by the Lockes.

Rayne had berated Potter all the way through the short journey for leaving the despondent family to fend for themselves, but Potter was an accomplished survivor, hardened by long arduous military campaigns. He was not prepared to jeopardise his own meticulous planning, especially for one who donned the colours of the South.

Rayne was also worried and nervously concerned by what she had heard from the Lockes. Potter worked hard to reassure his wife that they were in no danger. He explained to her again, as he had on many occasions, that it was extremely rare for Indians to attack. He told her the convoy must have been unwelcoming, and he emphasized they must have provoked the Indians by being ignorant to their unusual ways and they must have been hostile towards them.

He added that many malicious and exaggerated tales were spread by travellers because it was often themselves who, being scared at the sight of the strange-looking redskins, attacked and killed first.

In any case, he confidently concluded, if the Lockes had been attacked, the Indians would just have taken whatever supplies they needed and fled far and quickly for fear of the US patrols and vigilantes.

Rayne was still unnerved, and she slept very little. Although they had made camp at the side of a chain of pines, she felt exposed by the way the wagon seemed to be lit up on the prairie by the clear sky and stars that seemed closer and gleamed with an unusual brilliance.

With nothing to shield the wagon on three sides, the wind began to moan and wail and throughout the long night, its gusts increased as it swept across the open landscape to beat against the canvas.

In the middle of the night, Potter had to stake the wagon to prevent it from turning by the force of the furious gales. Eventually, the wind abated enough for him to rest, but he too did not sleep well. He knew the Tennessean would not follow, but inwardly he was concerned with the report of the redskins' attack. He tried to dismiss the implausible tale, but for reassurance, he lay with a constant keen ear and both his rifle and LeMat fully loaded at his side.

By the time the Bromptons had arisen the following morning, the weather had dramatically changed and the sky was dull with heavy dark rain-threatening clouds.

With vision now impaired, Potter could not see the Lockes' camp through his binoculars so he tried to dismiss them from his thoughts as he began to pack up camp.

Lightning began to bellow, illuminating the dark horizon, and it wasn't long before the rain began to deluge upon them. He gave one last glance through his binoculars as the lightning flashed, but due to the shield of rain his vision was still obscured, and so finally he dismissed the Lockes to his past and reined his oxen into action.

With every mile they travelled the storm's ferocity increased and the ruts beneath their wheels began to moisten into a deep mire. The day's journey was wasted as the oxen struggled in the mud to find any grip and they skidded and slid as, lacking any adhesion, the wagon moved very slowly inch by inch in the unforgiving conditions.

Thunder now began to burst directly above them with repeated deafening reverberations and the gales increased as again they began to furiously sweep across the prairie and batter against the side of the wagon.

By midday it was almost impossible to travel. The wheel ruts were now water-filled trenches and, fearing injury to the animals, the Bromptons sought cover and shelter from the exposed fury of the elements in a small nestle of tall sycamores. Rayne managed to strike up a fire from the emergency dry wood stock whilst Potter secured the cow and oxen.

Disheartened from the barrage in the sky above and still reflecting on the harrowing report issued by Brody Locke, both the Brompton's felt absolute solitude drop upon them as they scanned across the expanse of the battered plain.

Darkness fell earlier than normal and with little to do, they ate promptly and decided to retire early. Potter sat by the fire smoking his pipe as he waited for Rayne to bed down. He smoked and watched the mesmerising flames and listened to the rain hiss on the heat a little longer than usual, and he was just about to turn out the tobacco from his pipe into his hand and dampen the embers when out of the rustling shadows stepped a dark figure.

Potter's chest moved neither in nor out as subconsciously, his whole body locked rigid and he held his breath as, emerging out of the dark foliage and into the dull orange firelight, was an assured striding, solitary Indian warrior.

Potter shuddered, not from the cold rain, but from apprehension as alarm escalated within him.

The tall and bold Indian did not look at Potter, instead he strode past his side and lowered himself near the warmth of the fire.

The orange glow lightened the warrior and although he was wet, his breeches and leggings were not soaked and so Potter surmised he had been watching the Brompton's activities from the seclusion and protection of the pines and sycamores. Potter's legs succumbed to a slight tremble as he rested his hand on the butt of his LeMat.

"How di Chi," said the Indian without looking away from the flames. Potter understood the greeting, 'Hello man,' but he said nothing in response.

The warrior leaned nearer to the flames and crouched, with his heels touching the back of his thighs, then he held out his open hands to the warmth of the fire.

"Ma... fud...biskit...korphee," he grunted, this time nodding his head towards the wagon and rubbing his fingers close up to his lips. Again, Potter knew enough of the native language to translate 'Woman, food, biscuits, and coffee'.

He knew that within the redskins' society it was hospitable for the females to host all the requirements of the male, but without removing his right hand from the pistol, Potter raised his left palm to the side of his cheek and, slanting his head, he answered, "Sleep."

Then he shook his head to deny the Indian's request.

In the dimness Potter noticed the Indian open his eyes wide then narrow them again as he sniffed and gulped in the remnant odours of the evening meal as around them, the silence was only broken by the continual gusts of wind, the rustling of the trees, and the rain splattering down into the mud around them.

Potter slowly stretched close to the Indian to offer his pipe.

Enlarging his yellow eyes and exhaling a grunt, the Indian stopped rubbing his hands in the warmth and reached out to accept the amber glowing piece.

Although accustomed to the ways of the natives, Potter was not at ease. He gulped with trepidation, as the fire revealed the red shimmer of mesquite dye and sable braids of hair which fell down both sides of the man's half black-painted, rain-smudged face.

He was able to study the warrior. He was shirtless, but he wore a breechcloth and deerskin leggings with moccasins to match. Hanging across his shoulder was a US Army rifle, and tucked in a leather pouch was a large hunting knife. It was at this point Potter knew the warrior was not from the native Arapaho, but from the dreaded Lakota tribe and that the Brompton's lives were in peril.

His thoughts were in turmoil, but he knew he must not show any signs of fear as the Lakota only respected bravery. Potter glanced around the edge of the camp and towards the trees. He sensed other eyes upon him. The sound of his pipe exploding in the flames snapped him out of his trance-like state. The Indian had discarded the pipe into the flames and again he moved his fingers to his mouth to indicate he was hungry.

"Fud. Git mi fud."

Potter remained unmoved, but a slight tremble in his legs began to irk him.

"Fud! Me want muur." The warrior repeated loudly, this time banging his chest with a clenched fist to indicate he was becoming impatient.

Startling both men, the wagon canvas was thrown back and Rayne appeared carrying a well-stocked basket which she held out for Potter to pass onto the intruder.

She had not been asleep, she was too uneasy to relax. The affair with the Locke's had not been pleasant, and it was against her beliefs and nature to leave the family to struggle in such dire circumstances. Her anxiety had not been eased by Potter's words of comfort and assurance and with the additional howling wind rocking the wagon and the flashes of lightning whitening her inner eyelids she had been unable to rest in peace.

She had heard the brief words of the Indian from beyond the canvas and she had acted without hesitation.

The warrior grabbed at the basket and as he inspected the contents Potter reached out and grabbed a wooden keg which he levelled towards the Indian.

"Whisky," he offered, "good whisky."

"Ah gid whikay." The redskin repeated and with a nod his stern poise eased and he released a teeth-baring huge smile.

Fully raising, and standing four inches above Potter, the warrior nodded a couple more times down at Potter, then he turned his back and disappeared into the blackness as quickly as he had first appeared, taking the keg with him.

Both the Brompton's drew a deep breath and sighed with relief simultaneously. Potter was sure the Indian's eyes contained a message to indicate the offerings had ensured they would not be intruded upon again, but before he moved, he looked into the darkness again and he hesitated as he contemplated his next action. Maybe he was just searching the Indian's eyes and demeanour for a sign of hope that did not exist.

He deliberately offered the whisky in the expectation the savages would revel in the spirit and sleep the night away, blissfully drunk.

Rayne threw a numbed glance at her husband. She feared their ordeal was not yet over. Still concerned for their safety, he nodded towards her and feigned a smile. He was, however, relieved his plan had worked.

He wasted no time by kicking out the flames and hurrying to clasp his arms tight around his wife. He held her shaking body firm, and they held the embrace as the blackness continued to be shattered by intermittent flashes of brilliance above them.

"Are we moving on?" Rayne desperately needed to hear her husband answer 'Yes'.

"No. We must remain stoic and show these damnable savages no fear." Potter tightened his embrace. "He will not return and we will not be attacked."

"I'd rather us move on." She was fearfully honest.

"You must not give vent to your feelings. Stay strong." He positioned Rayne so that he could look into her eyes and display to her his confident resolve. "We've set things straight with him, and they will leave us in peace if we stay firm. If we go now, they will think we are running away because we are hiding something more than a few belongings."

He pulled her tight against his body again as another flash of illumination, followed immediately by a thunderous clap, erupted above them.

"We must not show fear. They will respect us if we hold firm and stay true to our beliefs."

This time Potter took his wife's hand and led her into the wagon and eased her down onto the mattress. Lying by her side, he failed to offer her more support and comfort as he resorted to and relied upon the only true method of reassurance he knew, clasping tight in his right hand the LeMat while his rifle rested close by his left.

He lay as motionless as possible on his back with eyes staring upwards as his fingers stroked the engraving on the LeMat.

He felt out the serial number 428 over and over with his index finger whilst all the time he studied the sounds and flashes beyond the canvas, knowing this would be the longest sleepless night he had ever experienced. He sensed the wagon was being watched at every moment, but yet he felt totally alone.

With the first vestiges of the dawning light breaking through the low clouds, the Brompton's impatiently arose. Neither of them had slept through the long and tortuous night.

They had listened to every canvas-flapping gust of wind and the relentless rustling from the trees which had been accompanied by eye-blinding flashes of lightning which split the darkness and on several occasions gave rise to human silhouettes which seemed to appear and disappear with equal speed.

It was the worst night of both their lives and one which more than equalled the fear of battle for Potter.

To their relief, nothing from the camp had been disturbed or stolen and within minutes of rising the camp was packed up and, ignoring breakfast hunger pangs, they were once more on their westward journey towards, and into, the huge mountain-covered forests. Potter did notice several footprints in the mud as he attached the oxen, but he chose not to disclose this information to his wife.

Gratification washed over them equally but they were apprehensive as they sought to get miles between themselves and the camp and for the first time in the journey they yearned for the company of fellow emigrants.

Again, the travelling was hindered by the thick mud and occasional fallen trees which had to be dragged from the trail by the oxen, all of which added to the delay and further increased the Brompton's anxiety.

However, by midday the dingy clouds had drifted east and the sun's rays finally began to warm the cold faces of the worried travellers.

Instead of walking alongside the oxen as she normally did, Rayne had sat up on the travel board with her arm tightly linked around that of her husband.

Conversation did not flow easily and their thoughts were occupied with conjecture of the last few hours and what they had left behind them.

After travelling five hours without food or rest, replenishment was needed and although the Brompton's had not travelled clear of the thick woodlands altogether, they agreed that enough ground had been covered to permit them to take a safe and undisturbed rest.

On empty stomachs and in a tired, emotional state they decided they had suffered enough of the bone-grating and sickness-induced rocking motion for a while. The bumping over roots and ploughing through deep watery hollows could wait and so the Brompton's and their animals succumbed to a weary halt as they pulled up for a much-needed rest.

As was the usual practice, Rayne assembled rocks, and again using dry kindling from the wagon to ignite the flames, she began to heat coffee whilst Potter positioned grain bags for the cow and oxen. The smell of bacon and coffee soon called for Potter to hanker down close by the fire and whilst the talk was still sparse and their enthusiasm subdued, they began to relax and eat.

The first indication something was wrong was when Potter heard loud hissing from the direction of the fire.

He leaned over to his left and peered out beyond the thick trunk of a blue spruce to shoot a worried glance toward the camp.

Dread immediately descended over him and in his hurry to replace his manhood within his pants, he continued to urinate all over his feet and down the inside of his trousers. He pulled up his braces and sped back towards camp with his eyes frantically digesting the scene in front of him.

Eight redskins had emerged from the forest and had stealthily encroached around Rayne with silent, fleeting footsteps. The initial shock caused her to drop the coffee pot into the flames which was followed by a piercing scream.

Potter's startled eyes flickered with speed in all directions to assess the scene of imminent danger. His fear intensified when he saw a savage at the edge of camp holding their horses.

With their heads painted white, eyes circled black, and noses painted red, he immediately knew these intruders were from the same tribe as the previous night's visitor. At that moment, he knew the hated and dreaded Lakota raiders had followed them.

His eyes locked onto his rifle, which was propped against the wagon wheel, but on a small keg next to Rayne was his LeMat.

Nearing to within ten feet of the Lakota, he had seen enough to realise that they were at severe risk of a torturous death at the expense of the Indians' fun and the past retributions they served upon the white race.

Most of the men were bare-chested, with some wearing breechcloths to cover their groins, whilst a few of the others were clad in leather leggings. All had black and white painted faces and feathers fixed to their red-dyed hair, with the exception of one who drew Potter's attention. This Indian had tilted on his head a grey Confederate Kepi. Now within touching distance of the invaders, Potter recognised this Indian to be the same man who entered their camp the previous evening. Some of the Indians crouched down to form a semicircle around the fire, but the Kepi wearer stood erect and looked down at Potter.

"Fud. Wiskay!" he hissed, breathing alcohol into Potter's face, his eyes narrowed and his mouth curled as he released a satanic grin.

At this point, Potter's eyes fixed on the silver daisy chain that was hanging around the Indian's neck. Potter glanced sideward, and he saw Rayne's mouth drop ajar as she, too, had noticed the jewellery.

They exchanged a knowing look.

"They've traded it with Brody," he mouthed to her. "Just stay calm and it will be okay."

"Fud. Whikay. Na'ow!"

This time the Indian pushed Potter's chest, and he stumbled backward. He heard one of the Indians laughing insanely, and he saw Rayne smash her hand down to knock away the seated Indian's hand just as he was in the process of lifting her dress to peep up at her thighs.

The Brompton's preassembled offerings for occasions like this were almost exhausted, and Potter defied the instruction.

"No. It's all gone."

One of the squat Indians took the bacon pan, sniffed, and slid his fingers across its greasy surface, then he licked off the fat.

"Gudd... Muur," he shouted over his shoulder.

"Nothing left." Potter manoeuvred Rayne behind him and shielded her with his arm. "It's all gone. Understand? Nothing left!"

92

"Li'ar," shouted back the Kepi wearer.

"No. All gone. We have nothing. Now go!" Potter hailed, pointing towards their horses.

"Yu Li'ar," the Indian repeated, and he stepped sideward to move up very close to Rayne, who was panting hard for breath.

He smiled, looking down at her chest rising and falling, then he put his face next to her cheek and sniffed the back of her neck as, at the same time, he twirled her blond ringlets around his walnut-coloured fingers.

Her face twisted with disgust as the smell of rough living pierced her nostrils, and she pulled back as, at the same moment, Potter angled himself so he stood between them again, with his face replacing that of his wife's.

"Ni'ce yella harr."

Both men's eyes locked on each other's, and they held the staring position without blinking. The Lakota man's eyes narrowed. Beads of sweat began to roll down Potter's forehead, but both gazes remained firm and unmoved until Rayne screamed out again.

"No! No! Get out!"

The call ended the strength of the mind struggle as Potter glanced over his shoulder to see that one of the Indians had climbed up onto the schooner. He held his wife tight to prevent her from trying to stop the intruder, but as he was momentarily distracted, another Indian grabbed Rayne's dress and began to pull her away from his grasp.

Releasing Rayne to the drag of the Indian, Potter dived towards his LeMat. He scrambled in the mud to clasp his shaking hand around the walnut handle and, within the same movement, he drew up onto his knees to take aim at the attacker.

He now knew his final breaths of life would soon be cast, but he was still not prepared to allow the redskins to see his fear, and he was not prepared to yield and be savaged without a fight.

The the sight of his wife being accosted had ignited him with a retaliatory fury that could not be contained.

A loud explosion of noise erupted as the LeMat unleashed its force with full success, and the velocity of the buckshot burst open the accosting Indian's chest and threw his body high and backward.

His hand went limp, and releasing his grip on Rayne, the Indian's lifeless body splashed hard into the mud.

Before the orange bellow of flame had died out from the barrel of the LeMat, the Kepi wearer had smashed the butt of his rifle hard against Potter's cheekbone. Immediately, half of Potter's face caved inward, and he fell to his knees.

Intense pain blocked out his vision, and everything before him spun in a distorted, colourless, thick haze.

Rayne was deranged by fear, and she screamed out her husband's name repeatedly as she swung out her frenzied arms in a bid to reach her prostrate husband.

Potter managed to raise his head, and he squinted hard enough to see another Indian barge into Rayne to stop her from nearing him and hurl her onto her back. Although in a perilous state, Potter was just able to fathom the demonic scene around him. To his front, a few yards away, his wife was being molested again by two more Indians, and to the side his belongings and supplies were being tossed down into the mud from the schooner.

The Kepi wearer above him was performing a tribal chant and so, with a gut-wrenching almighty effort, he drew one long deep breath and tried hard to focus through his only functioning eye. He filled his lungs with air and began to level the LeMat but, just as he took aim at one of Rayne's blurry attackers, he felt an almighty paralysing pain burn right through his back.

The chanting Kepi wearer had driven his spear straight through Potter and weighted his shoulder behind the force and speed, so the iron head crushed its way through sinew, organs, and bone until it bore deep into the mud.

Not satisfied with its destruction, the Lakotan applied more pressure and twisted hard on the spear until Potter was pinned to the ground and unable to break free.

He screamed as the intense pain burst from head to foot, but only gurgled blood was emitted from his mouth. To his front he was just able to see Rayne's eyes expand in horror as, fighting off her attackers, she glimpsed the sight of her husband's agony, which overwhelmed her with more pain from within.

Potter bit hard against his teeth to abate the pain just enough to permit him one last act of defiance, and he again took aim, but this time, as he squinted hard and squeezed on the trigger, the only sound he heard was the blade of an axe chopping through his wrist.

Briefly, before his mind relented into blackness, he saw his detached hand still gripping tight to the blood-covered LeMat.

The last sound Potter heard was the terrified screams for mercy from Rayne as the Lakotans began to tear away at her clothing.

Rayne frantically fisted and scratched at her attackers, but the last vision she would ever see through her water-filled eyes was that of the Kepi wearer pulling back Potter's head and sliding the blade of his knife across her unconscious husband's forehead. She did not see the savage in front of her expose his genitalia, nor did she feel him rip off her bloomers and force himself upon her as seeing the Kepi wearer peeling her husband's scalp back overwhelmed her, and she succumbed to a silent and peaceful oblivion.

Kepi ignored the rape and pillage surrounding him. He was fastening Potter's scalp to his belt when his gaze and attention dropped down to the severed hand clutching around the LeMat.

He crouched lower to inspect the weapon, and he held the arched position momentarily before releasing a satisfied smile as, reaching down, he raised the trophy out from the pool of blood.

Laughing insanely as Potter's rigid hand failed to release its grip from the walnut, he waved the LeMat and the flapping hand in the direction of the rapists.

Chapter 4

September 24th, 1867

The six outlaws, Alexander Franklin James, Jesse Woodson James, Clell Miller, Bob Foston, John Jarret, and George Washington Sheppard, were hankered down enclosing the roaring campfire. The sky was cloudless and black and so the night air had cooled to an unpleasant chill. Discontentment was brewing within a couple of members of the gang.

"You grunt some shit, Clell." Sheppard derided as he tore some measly strands of meat from a flamed squirrel.

"Ah, shut your mouth, you one-eyed runt." Clell's retort was direct and Sheppard's long moustache dropped sidewards as his face firmed, his forehead rutted, and he frowned at Clell.

"I'm with Clell. I want us to get back to our original plan." Added Foston, as he too was salvaging what he could eat from a roasted prairie squirrel.

"Yeah, get back to helping ourselves to Union coffers and causing as much havoc on those murderous Democrat bastards as we can." Clell was buoyed by Bob's support.

"Quit ya jabbering, Clell." Said Jesse through the flames.

98

"You've gotten all soft in that Union jail and you're just not used to saddlery no more… that's all."

Clell had been captured by Union forces while fleeing the failed attack on Albany, and he spent the remainder of the Civil War, and much of his youth in a prisoner-of-war camp.

Although his young age earned him relatively kind treatment from both the Union guards and his fellow Confederate prisoners, he still resented Jesse and Frank, believing they could have helped him escape the battlefield instead of focusing solely on saving themselves when the raid on the Union-occupied town collapsed.

"Stop yer teasing, Dingus."

Immediately Clell knew he should not have used the derogatory term as it was sure to ignite a reaction from Jesse's fiery temper and within the same instant a carbon-wood stick Jesse had been using to stoke up the fire was thrown across the flames, striking Clell hard on the chest.

"Say that again, Clell!" The insulting reference had originated from Jesse himself when a couple of years earlier he had been cleaning his pistol and he fired it by mistake, blowing off one of his fingers.

Remaining calm and showing no signs of pain, he casually said, "Well, ain't that the most dingus darndest thing." The term had stuck for a while as the gang's leader at the time, Archie Clement, used it to refer to the young Jesse.

However, now, with Archie dead, the mature and intolerant Jesse would not accept foolery at his expense from his considered subordinates within the gang he was now leading.

"Go on, Clell," Jesse continued, "I dare ya. Call me Dingus again."

Clell remained silent, his eyes avoiding all contact with Jesse. Instead, he looked at Frank as often the elder brother would intervene in situations like this and calm down his hot-headed sibling, but on this occasion, Frank seemed too occupied with his supper to pay any attention to the bickering.

"Well, come on, Clell. I dare ya. Say it again."

"Oh shucks, Jesse. I'm just sick of prairie doves and squirrels, that's all."

Clell referred to the recent weeks of travel hardship they had endured. Since the end of the Civil War, the young men from Missouri had been subjected to persecution and many difficult and testing times by their northern victors.

At the start of the amnesty, Jesse had been shot as he tried to surrender to the Union officials.

Then, as the young men around the blazing campfire had tried to return to their farms, they found they were unable to buy stocks at fair prices nor were they able to sell their goods because the Union citizenry heavily favoured the northern traders.

Allegiances were formed favouring the northern bias, ensuring that trading was not conducted on equal terms. Southern veterans and sympathisers suffered as they were unable to prosper from their toil.

Many Missourians were forced to sell off their lands and businesses to their northern competitors for less than value to enable them to flee west, but Archie Clements, Jesse, and Frank James had decided to rebel and challenge the authorities. Archie was soon killed and now leading the gang, the James brothers decided their families had suffered enough and they enrolled themselves as avenging bank robbers targeting only Union profiteering families and banks. In less than two years they had robbed four banks, but now additional Union forces had been assigned to capture or kill all rebel guerrillas, and so Jesse and Frank had decided to flee to Kansas and avoid the brutal suppression by taking the gang to Denver until the situation in Missouri had calmed.

"Well, alright, Clell, but if you ever call me Dingus again, I'll blow your God-darn nose right off your face."

At that moment Jesse cared little for the friendship which had bonded the two men all their lives. "You understand?"

"I think Clell's got a point, Jesse." Again Foston added support.

"Yeah. What's the point of us having all this Union money if we can't put anything good in our mouths and fatten our bellies?" Now Jarrett joined the dispute.

Frank had been shrewdly paying attention the whole time and now he chose to engage. "Look, boys, we can't go back just yet."

He was calm, but his deep voice presented authority. "Not whilst the Union disfranchisement is keeping all the honest folk from making a living and holding 'em down so low they're darn near starving to death."

"Surely, Frank, we'd be helping our folks better by turning back and doing what we did in Liberty and Lexington." Foston expressed, and then Clell added:

"You said we'd be okay for a while in Kansas and look how we had to skidaddle out of there."

"Yeah, and that shows how intent the new governor is with bringing us in." Frank knew the newly appointed Governor Thomas C. Fletcher would not rest until he had suppressed all the guerrillas' activities in Missouri.

"We will go back, but not just yet. Not until Fletcher is transferred. It's just not safe for us in Missouri yet. He will keep the state militia hunting us down until we are either filled with holes or we are swinging from our necks. Just like what they did with Payne Jones and Rich Burns… You ain't forgot about those two poor fellas, have ya boys?"

"You know I ain't, Frank, but we're not helping their families any by being this far out west sitting on our jacksies and near starving ourselves to death."

"Look, Clell. We just need to give it a couple more months, then we can get back to Missouri and cause enough revenge, havoc, and misery to make sure no one forgets the persecutions our families have been subjected to." Jesse stood to support his brother by justifying the gang's banditry. "We'll have a few weeks or so to rest up in Denver and fill ourselves with all the food our stomachs can hold."

"Booze. Can we have a little liberation?" Jarrett beseeched.

"Plenty, and take to obliging as many women as we can. Then we'll bleed it dry and get the hell out of this state with our noses dry so we can get back down to business in Missouri." Jesse settled.

"I just think that maybe we should have gone down to Texas with the Youngers." Clell continued.

"You wanna go with the Youngers, Clell?" Jesse was agitated. He stood up to stretch out his stiffening back and spanned out his fingers on his right hand. "Do ya?"

"Ain't nothing down in Texas aside from sweat, peppers, and Mexicans." Frank added, his eyes scrutinising Jesse's unrest. "Hellfire, Clell. I've heard you can't even tell the women from the men."

"Might suit Cole and Bob, but that ain't no use to me." Declared Jarrett with a hint of laughter.

Cole scowled at Jarrett. The comment had vexed him.

"Yeah. I hear even the whores have all got black mantle slugs draped across their top lips," Frank sneered as he glared, then winked at Jesse with a hint that he wanted the clash to end without bloodshed, "and burnsides to match."

"If it makes ya feel better, Clell, we can always take our next hiatus down there with Cole and Bob." Jesse relented to amiably ease the tension and within minutes the bandits nestled down on the ground to stare skywards until the shimmering speckles eased them into a comfortable slumber with their thoughts filled with gratification to come in Denver.

Dust arose in their wake with ease as the six outlaws galloped across the sun-baked, cracked prairie.

Up at dawn they had slowly ambled towards the Rockies in the distance, but after a midday break the small talk, challenging banter, and light frivolity had broken out into a race to reach a line of tall sycamores which expanded in their eyeline.

Bob Foston was twenty yards clear of the pack when he suddenly pulled his mount to an abrupt halt. Pulling up beside him, the outlaws stared across to the object which had captured Bob's attention.

"Worth a look?" he said, turning his head towards Frank for approval.

"Why not? Ain't seen anything but grass for a few days. Might be something to our liking in there." Frank replied, squinting hard at the abandoned schooner.

Veering off to their right, it soon became obvious to the riders the wagon had been discarded for a long time.

The wagon canvas, which flapped in the mild breeze, was ripped beyond repair and broken crates were strewn randomly across the knee-length grass.

Pulling up closer, the gang saw scattered partly clothed bones which were spread wide around the schooner. Silently, the riders dismounted to inspect the scene of desolation in more detail.

"What ya thinking?" Jesse asked Frank as he lowered to study the partial remains of a skeleton in a tattered dress.

"That's what I'm thinking." He answered, pointing to the previously unseen far side of the wagon.

Jesse arched sidewards to peer towards the area where Frank was pointing. His face twisted into an expression of shock and confusion as his eyes locked upon and focused in on five skulls that were impaled on makeshift wooden poles. The gang held mute as they apprehensively digested the barbarity.

"Redskins." Frank confirmed as he stood motionless directly in front of the horrifying line of skulls. He flattened his moustache between his thumb and finger and added, "See these marks?"

He raised a finger to the jagged marks on the foreheads of the skulls. "Poor blighters have been scalped."

"Jesus… Frank." Sheppard drew his six-shooter and squinted with his one eye in all directions. "You said nothing about redskins being out here."

Jarrett also drew his gun as the men's mood swiftly changed from being jovial and inquisitive to one of dreaded concern.

"Put 'em back, you muttonheads, and rest easy." Jesse reassured, turning open the palms of his hands. "Whoever did this has long since gone."

"Never seen a savage," said Jarrett, holstering his pistol.

"This must have happened months ago." Frank added, still inspecting the skulls and shaking his head.

"Coyotes will have ripped up and eaten whatever was left of the poor bastards." Said Jesse as he arched over another decimated skeleton.

He lifted the shredded shirt with a stick to see if there was a purse or wallet with identification and he noticed the ribs had been shattered by a mass of bullets which were still embedded in some of the bones.

"Look at this!" shouted Clell from the rear of the schooner. He held out in front of him a small decomposed baby, which was skewered on a spear.

"God darn, Clell." Frank shouted in dismay. "Get down and put a soil covering over the poor little son of a bitch."

"I think you should see this, Frank." Bob had also climbed into the back of the wagon with Clell and he held out a ripped and discoloured piece of paper he had found amongst the remains.

Frank carefully took the document from Bob and angled it towards the sun. Most of the ink was smudged and unreadable, but the bold heading was clearly legible and Frank read it out aloud.

"Confederate States of America. To whom it may concern that," he paused because the next words had faded almost beyond deciphering, "erm, Brody somebody," the name 'Locke' had faded beyond deciphering. "Captain of the regiment of something in Tennessee was enlisted on the twenty-seventh day of March, one thousand and eight hundred and sixty-two to serve for the war, is honourably discharged from the army of the Confederate States."

Frank scowled and shook his head. "Poor fella was one of our boys." He raised his head from the paper and added, "Come on, let's collect 'em all in and give 'em a holy burial only rightful for one of our fighting men and his loved ones."

"Sure in hell didn't deserve this." Jesse said, lifting the first of the bones from the ground.

Bob held out his left hand to Frank. "Look, Frank, there's more."

Carefully Frank took the pile of documents and carefully fingered his way through the decomposing collection of photographs, letters, worthless Confederate currency notes, and a captain's promotion certificate.

All were weather-damaged and too frail to inspect thoroughly, but on the back of a female portrait Frank could just make out the name 'Mattie'.

Anything of worth had already been pillaged or had rotted away so, joining the lamented gang, he laid the collection on top of the bones then he watched and said a small prayer as Jesse, Sheppard, and Jarrett covered the remains with rocks and a light covering of soil. Clell skilfully carved out a wooden plaque, which simply stated:

Brody and family

Honourable Confederate Captain

The group didn't rest easy or get much sleep that night. They made camp under the shelter of the sycamores and even though they took turns to keep watch, the prairie and forest nightlife kept disturbing all of them and little sleep was granted. They could not prevent their anxious and disturbed minds from tormenting them and plaguing them with thoughts of ghoulish demon visions.

Before the dawning sun had pierced through the forest canopy, the outlaws had broken camp and continued on their journey to Denver.

 They scaled their way up then back down the many steep inclines, crossed streams, with the only disturbance they encountered being from the rustling in the trees and the wildlife which scurried in retreat at the first sign of the approaching horsemen.

As the dimness began to set in on the twenty-third day of their journey, an orange glow in the distance persuaded the men to draw to a silent halt.

Surmising the fire was that of fellow travellers or hunters, they proceeded with caution, ensuring no signs of encroachment were made.

From a distance of about one hundred and fifty yards, the gang could see through the black timbers the campfire was far superior in size and vigour than that of an expected hunter or lonely traveller so they decided to secure their horses, laden themselves with weaponry, and make the final approach delicately on foot.

The smell of roasting meat began to overwhelm the usual pine fragrance as the six men edged towards the camp. The cautious approach proved a wise decision as, peering out of the darkness and through the thick wooden trunks, the Missourians had a clear, fire-illuminated view of eight face-painted Indians.

"Oh hell… I propose we turn back." Clell whispered.

"Just calm yourself, Clell. They're most probably local friendlies." Frank's eyes were attracted to the rotating deer above the flames.

The outlaws silently watched the relaxed Indians attending to the fire, preparing their food, passing around the pipe, and communicating meaningless chatter.

Jesse leant closer to Frank's ear. "See that."

Frank strained to focus on the orangey shadow figures.

"See what?" He could only see silhouettes warming their faces near the fire.

"There." Jesse pointed to one of the only two standing Indians. "Look. You see it?"

Frank's face screwed tighter, and he leant forward a little and lowered a branch silently with one finger to aid his view.

Jesse noticed Frank's frown release, and his eyes widened to indicate the brothers now had the same thoughts. "You thinking the same as me?"

"Believe so." Frank did not move his gaze from the Indian wearing the Confederate hat.

"It can't be no coincidence." Whispered Jesse.

"Don't think they could have traded it?" Frank suggested with an unconvincing tone.

"A Kepi?" Jesse was quick to dismiss.

"Erm, you're right." Frank paused for a moment as if he were considering the options, then he swivelled at the waist and beckoned with his arms for the gang to close in around him. "These savages are the butchers that murdered the Brody family back yonder."

"How do you know that, Frank?" Sheppard breathed.

"That tall son of a bitch over near the fire is wearing his candy." Frank leaned his head toward the fire.

The gang remained apprehensively silent. They knew Jesse was intent on executing vengeance at every opportunity whilst Frank was an unflappable natural killer and the brothers would be unable to resist confronting the menaces in front of them.

"What ya thinking, Frank?" Clell knew he didn't need to ask.

"I'm thinking we blast them all to Hell." He confirmed to Jesse's approving head bow and a matching huge grin.

The gang did not share the James brothers' natural fearlessness or their capacity for administering death without compassion.

Foston's and Jarrett's eyes flicked across at each other nervously. Clell's palms began to sweat and Sheppard's mouth suddenly dried.

The gang needed a few minutes to summon their composure, but Jesse sensed the apprehension surrounding him and, so undaunted, he decided to act and rise from the kneeling position.

"Come on, fellas. Let's do this for Captain Brody and his poor kinfolk." He whispered, as at the same time, he carefully slid his pistol out from the holster.

The perceptive Kepi wearer's face stoned and his eyes glanced toward the darkness on his left side. He tilted his head slightly as if to improve his hearing and he concentrated on the unfamiliar noise in the shrubs.

He alone heard the isolated snap beyond the perimeter of the camp and his suspicions had been roused, but it was too late and his inquisitive gaze was greeted with an illuminating flash and the thunderous eruption of relentless pistol and rifle discharge.

Blood and bark burst in all directions as yells and screams of pain smothered the thudding sound of lead propelling through flesh and the shattering of bones.

Most of the Indians fell instantly to the ground as death dictated their only movement, but the Kepi wearer and another Indian instinctively reacted by charging toward their assailants with retaliatory rifle fire.

Stepping forwards out of the trees and the thick powdered smog, the outlaws continued to unleash their fire without remorse or pity and only the Kepi wearer remained on his feet longer than a few seconds.

Staggering forwards with possessed determination and ignoring all pain and blood which spurted from the four holes in his chest, he swung his axe threateningly at Frank, but stumbling to within almost touching distance Frank had remained calm and he held his arm straight with his barrel levelled at the unobstructed face when he pulled again on the trigger.

One last blast erupted and lead bore deep into the Indian's skull, thrusting his head back and his dead body to the ground.

For a long moment, the outlaws stood motionless in the low-hanging smog with their irons hanging by their side. They scanned in all directions for signs of movement and their ears were alert and intent upon alarming if any unusual noises were to be detected.

"Where's Bob?" Sheppard said, looking both left and right.

"What?" Frank heard Sheppard, but he answered instinctively.

"Foston. Where the hell is he?" Sheppard repeated his alarm.

"He's down here." Jesse hollered, re-entering the thick foliage.

"Bob... Bob. You injured?"

Within seconds Jesse, Frank, and Sheppard were all arched in a curve around the unmoving darkened figure of Bob Foston.

"Bob… Bob!" Frank had struck up a match and lowered the glow over Bob's colourless face.

With his head arched back, his face held a pained grimace. His eyes were half closed and blood drooled from the side of his mouth.

Jesse faintly shook Bob by the shoulders and called his name again but only dead breath was discharged from Bob's lungs. He had not seen the outlaws' extermination of the Indians as a retaliatory Indian bullet had punctured his heart, killing him instantly.

Remaining oblivious to Bob's demise, Clell neared and examined the Kepi wearer. He launched his boot into the Indian's rib cage but only the last breath of the Indian was forced out. He looked over to Jarrett, who was checking the Indians to his left.

Clell noticed one of the dead had fallen face forward into the fire and he decided to pull the scorched body from the flames before the cremation smell sickened his stomach, but as he began to move a glint from the fire flashed from the Kepi wearer's belt. He paused and held the position for a second look.

"Well, I'll be darned." He whispered to himself as, reaching down, he wrapped his fingers around the walnut handle of a LeMat pistol. "Good God almighty." He grinned as his animated eyes marvelled at the piece as he angled it from side to side in the light from the fire. "Gonna be getting me some lead for this beauty."

"What you got there, Clell?" Jesse shouted, coming up behind him.

Clell did not answer. His relish had been disturbed as he saw Frank and Sheppard carrying the limp body of Bob out from the darkness.

Chapter 5

September 7th, 1876

"I'm sorry for getting ya into this, Jim," Cole said quietly to his brother.

The Younger brothers were riding side by side, twenty yards or so behind and out of earshot of the rest of the gang.

"This place bodes ill," Cole whispered.

"Don't matter none to me, Cole. Northfield or Mankato, a bank is a bank and money is money, and besides, I haven't done anything that can't be altered," Jim replied to his older brother.

Cole Younger had written to his younger sibling a few months earlier, urging him to leave his farm in California to rejoin the gang for another bank robbery.

Cole and his younger brother Bob had wanted to raid either Mankato or Garden City, but Jesse and Frank were insistent upon heading further north and deep into Minnesota to raid a Union-backed repository in Saint Peter.

During the final stakeout, Frank became hesitant and felt uneasy, so the James brothers convinced the gang to raid the First National Bank in Northfield.

Cole knew that Clell, Bill Chadwell, and Charlie Pitts were perpetually loyal to the James brothers, and so he hoped by bringing Jim back into the gang he may have been able to swing Jesse and Frank's judgement, and the opinions of Bill and Charlie, to opt for robbing the Garden City bank, which was Cole's first choice.

The Younger brothers had always stuck together and never turned their backs on each other. They had been raised that way and, with Jim being well respected by all the gang members, including Jesse, something which Cole failed to do, Cole had hoped his brother could sway the gang's opinions regarding which bank to rob.

Over the past few weeks, whilst the gang were conducting their surveillance, the relationship between the gang leaders had deteriorated to the point where they now began to avoid each other. Both men knew if an argument flared, their impatience would be ignited and, with both men holding an unnatural fear of death, either one of them or both would be killed.

However, Jim's arrival did little to alter the bandits' opinions. Their minds were set on raiding the larger bank, which had an assured substantial wealth which, unfortunately for Cole, Jim also favoured.

"I've got a bad feeling today, Jim. I'm sick as a knocked-up whore with Jesse and his domineering ways. After today, I'm taking my loot and splitting down to Texas for good," Cole confided.

"Look at him riding up front all the darn time. Dumb mule head thinks he's George Armstrong Custer." He cussed.

For the last six weeks, the outlaws had been in continual disagreement about which bank to hold up next.

Their careers as robbers had flourished with success when they returned from Denver. In nine years, they had inflicted financial pain and human loss throughout Missouri, Iowa, and Kentucky. They had robbed over eight banks, four trains, and numerous stagecoaches, each time managing to evade the Union militia and slip away into anonymity with ease until they reassembled after a few weeks' rest to strike again.

However, now a task force of Pinkerton National Detective Agency operatives had been assigned to eliminate the Jesse James and Cole Younger gang, and they were now beginning to find it difficult to secure safe houses and hideouts in Missouri.

Their neighbours and friends had been turned by fear of retribution, and they no longer welcomed the vigilantes on their lands and in their homes.

Jesse and Frank rode up front with Clell, Bob Younger, Charlie, and Bill close in behind.

"Well, fellas," Jesse hollered over his shoulder, "I don't figure on raising hell much longer than I have to."

Contemplation for the future on the long ride had lingered in Jesse's thoughts, and he too was beginning to feel sceptical now he could not find safe refuge in Missouri.

Mistrust had crept upon him, and he no longer looked at his dependable compatriots in the same trusted way. Reward money impelled temptation for the poor and lawless, and vengeance had been unleashed on the James gang's kin by the northern regulators.

"What in darnation are you talking about?" Frank asked his brother.

Cole and Jim's eyes locked on each other, and they wondered if somehow Jesse had heard them talking and if the comment was in riposte to Cole's backbiting.

"You heard me, Frank. As soon as I've got me enough Yankee dough to sit me comfortable, I'm going to settle down with Zee somewhere well away from Missouri and ride out the rest of my days as a wealthy, law-abiding citizen."

"You mean that, Jesse?" Clell asked, almost as if his ears were deceiving him.

"I sure do, Clell."

"I know Zee did plenty more than just raise you back to health." Frank smiled with the quip regarding his cousin Zerelda and her techniques for nursing Jesse back to full health after he was shot by the Union soldiers. "But I never thought she'd tampered with your mind."

He ignored his brother's teasing. "I ain't been much of a husband, but I reckon after today I'll have me enough financial security to make Zee an honest, respectable woman."

"Why, you wicked little hornet," Frank teased, "planning on a different type of riding... eh, Jesse?"

"Been giving it a lot of thought, Frank. Times are moving on, and I'm thinking it's time I did the same." He tipped back his hat slightly to refresh his face with the bright midmorning sunlight. "I'm thinking we're now in the wrong line of work," he drew in a breath of the crisp September air, "and I'm thinking you boys should do the same."

"What you talking about, Jesse?" Bill rode up beside Jesse after only hearing part of the conversation.

"Find an alternative profession. Complete a different line of work, Bill."

"What about avenging the death of Archie?" shouted Bob Younger from the rear.

"I figure we've all done enough for poor Archie, and besides, I've already tasted one Yankee bullet and I ain't figuring on taking another from those God darn Pinct's," Jesse replied.

"Well, I for one, ain't done yet with what Archie started." Clell looked around for support from Charlie and Bob, who were now riding close to his side.

Neither of them spoke, and the silence was cut by Jesse before Clell had time to further comment. "Well, I'll tell you what, Clell. I'll pay my homage to Archie whilst I'm sitting comfy with my pipe and slippers."

"Darn Pinkerton's will keep on hunting you down, Jesse. They're predators, and the Government will make sure their eagerness will not wane."

"You sure about that, Frank?" hollered Cole from the rear. "B'cos I hear there is an amnesty coming for us all."

"What?" Jesse pulled his horse to a sudden halt, which blocked the pathway.

"That's right, Jesse. I read it in the State Herald." Cole went on. "To bring an end to our ways, they're gonna offer us all an amnesty."

"You believe that nonsense, Cole?" Jesse asked with a challenging tone, turning his horse to face his cousin.

122

“I believe it is coming.”

Cole remained firm and glared forward at Jesse and beyond the horse riders, who were all groomed in their new long dusters to resemble cattlemen.

“They're all full well thinking we ain’t never gonna stop from making them Yankees pay for all the torment and suffering they’ve laid on our families, so they're figuring they’ve no option but to offer us a full amnesty.”

“Well, just you keep on trying to believe that, Cole, but you know as well as I do the only amnesty we’ll ever see will be in the hereafter when you’ve been planted like manure,” Jesse replied, turning his horse forward to scan the way ahead. “It ain’t ever going to happen,” he motioned his horse to continue onwards. “So for now, Cole, you need to clear out all that shit and nonsense and just remember it ain’t hard to get yourselves shot.” Jesse then shouted over his other shoulder, “And you boys all need to think hard about that too.”

“Or to make a mistake,” Cole quipped through gritted teeth, still irked by Jesse’s choice of bank, but his comments fell unheard as the tempo increased and the clopping of hooves covered his words.

Seemingly searching for some encouragement, Clell reached down and withdrew his LeMat.

He released a pleased smile and recalled how his find all those years back had been the envy of all the gang.

He held it up to the sunrays, but now it failed to glisten. His distressed wife's saddened face and her serene acceptance on the day she saw him remove the LeMat from the bedroom drawer flashed into his thoughts, dispelling his enthusiasm.

"You thinking of using that old pepper pot?" Frank grinned.

"Hellfire, Clell," Jesse glanced to his rear and laughed, "you definitely ought to retire back to your mule farm if you're relying on that iron for your salvation."

"Naw, fellas. Just b'cos I ain't used it for a while don't mean it can't despatch a storm, and besides... I've figured farming ain't right for me," Clell replied, cloaking the weapon.

"How's that?" asked Jesse.

"I'm sick to the guts of shovelling up shit, and with my share, I'm going to buy me a nice little saloon and I'm going to fill it to the rafters with herdy girls."

Jesse spliced the eruption of laughter. "Whilst you boys are listening," he glanced backwards, "I'm telling you, fellas, this here bank is fat with cash."

Frank cut in and added, "Yeah, fat with Yankee cash stolen from good southern Christian folks."

"That's right, Frank, and I'm telling you all when we've filled our bags with this bona fide Yankee dough, there'll be enough to go around and settle us up for life. No more shovelling mule shit, Clell, and hats off to the herdy girl saloon!" howled Jesse as he pulled off his hat and slapped it down hard on his horse's rear.

"Well, are you boys just gonna wag ya tongues all day?" Frank followed up, pulling away at speed. "Or are we going to load ourselves up with some of that cash!"

With an almost collective eagerness and laughter, the rest of the outlaws heeled their horses to an increased stride to leave only dust in their wake as they urged on with an excitable urgency towards Northfield.

By midday, the eight riders pulled to a halt on the bank of the Cannon River. The citizens of Northfield, only yards away, were routinely and innocently performing their normal daily activities on this warm late summer's day.

"One last time," Jesse began.

"Oh, stop all of your shitting, Jesse. We've been over this already," Cole moaned, recalling the ritual nightly planning discussions about the roaring campfires.

"Look, Cole! I know the folk around here ain't as cautious as in Missouri."

The way Jesse rapidly and repeatedly blinked irked Cole, and he wasn't paying any attention or listening to Jesse's sermon.

On the final approach to Northfield, he too had decided this would be the last time he would ever ride with the James gang, and his thoughts were now of a new beginning in faraway Texas.

"Even though Bill's already confirmed this place is full of dumb farmers and yellow-bellied businessmen, I don't want to leave anything to chance," Jesse continued, knowing Cole's thoughts were engaged elsewhere, and he scowled. "I want no mistakes."

He turned to pull his horse alongside Cole. "You hear me? I want us in and out with our haul and no one getting left behind."

Jesse's mind was fully absorbed with the mission ahead, and he was now consumed with a volatile appetite for reigning terror and fear deep into the hearts of the Union nationals.

All night he had walked through the events of the robbery in his mind, and he had no patience for any criticisms or commentary.

The gang, and especially Cole, were accustomed to his ways, and they knew it was wise not to say anything. They had seen his personality transform this way on many occasions, especially just before a robbery, when the tension was intense.

"I just want to get on with it, Jesse," Cole admitted. "I've travelled over four hundred miles and my legs have gone to sleep and my arse is sore."

"Charlie, Jim, and Bill, you're staying on the bridge to cut the telegraph wires and guard our escape." Jesse ignored Cole. "Make sure the bridge is clear, then when you see us coming out, be ready to lead us out of Northfield and to safety."

"Don't you worry any, Jesse. I know every slough, every tree, and —"

"Every whorehouse!" Bob cut in and shouted out to immediate laughter, which eased the tension.

Bill shook his head and released a hint of a grin, which matched the sudden flush in his cheeks, and then he waited for their enjoyment to settle before he finished.

"And every trail in these woods better than any lawman in Minnesota."

Jesse only acknowledged Bill's boast with a nod. He hadn't joined in with the laughter, and he had no desire for any needless banter.

"Cole, Clell, you two—"

"Yeah, yeah, yeah, Jesse," Cole cut in, confirming he was fully aware of the plan. "We're gonna pull up outside the bank at two o'clock and make sure that you, Frank, and Bob get the hell out. The plan's crystal, Jesse, and we all know what we've gotta do."

Jesse's eyes narrowed to reveal his displeasure for Cole's contempt, but he decided on this occasion to ignore his cousin's bold affront.

"Right, I'll see you at two outside Lee and Hitchcock's goods store." He said, pulling out and glancing down at his timepiece.

"Just one thing, Jesse." Cole cut in.

"Yeah. What will that be, Cole?" Jesse's face creased as he manufactured a smile to hide his irritation.

"Nobody gets hurt today."

"What?" Jesse's head tilted slightly.

"You heard me, Jesse."

"Oh, I heard you alright, Cole... loud and clear." He swung his horse around so that he faced the gang. "Listen up, you boys. Don't you go shooting anybody today because Cole here doesn't like it anymore."

Then, replacing his watch inside his coat pocket, he declared, "All right now. It's straight up one o'clock. Come on, Frank, Bob, let's go get us some breakfast."

128

With these words of finality, Jesse James heeled his horse into motion and onto the bridge to cross over the Cannon River.

One hour later, Cole and Clell cantered over the bridge and onto Water Street.

"Holy… Lord of Lords… Northfield is busy today," Clell apprehensively said to Cole, as he observed the alarming and unexpected number of public citizens.

"Yep, and as sure as it's hot in hell, old Dingus didn't plan for this. Darn fool should have ridden straight through town and swung around to call it off," Cole replied, drawing a deep breath to compose himself.

He began to feel unusually anxious, but he couldn't ride out and leave Northfield because his brother Bob was still with Jesse and Frank. He had no doubt that Jesse would stubbornly proceed with the plan, so he faked a smile, tilted his hat to a passerby in the street, and continued the approach along Water Street.

Without raising suspicion, Cole and Clell scanned the surrounding area. The boardwalks were heavily occupied. To their right, a few couples strolled hand in hand and were enjoying the sun. Reaching and crossing Mill Square, in front of them about one hundred yards away, they could see Jesse's, Frank's, and Bob's horses tied between Elred's confectionary and Lee and Hitchcock's dry goods store.

Clell pulled down the brim on his hat to shield his eyes from the glare of the sun as the pair slowly continued the short journey past the mill and the assembly of hardware, merchants, tailors, and grocery shops until they pulled to a halt outside the dry goods store alongside the First National Bank.

Dismounting next to the other three outlaws' horses, Cole sat on a crate whilst Clell lit up his pipe and casually leant on the horse rail.

After less than one minute, Jesse led the way out of Vintor's restaurant. He patted his stomach with the flat of both his hands, expressing a look of satisfaction, and crossed the track to the bank. He nodded in Cole's and Clell's direction as he footed the few steps up to the sidewalk.

Bob and Frank followed closely behind, replacing and adjusting their hats and coats. Cole slid from the crate and moved to the side of his horse where he started to feign adjusting the girth on his saddle.

He attempted to catch Bob's attention with a low-toned whistle, but Bob's eyes were focused on the nearing bank doorway.

Clell heard Cole mutter, "Darn it… God damn," under his breath as he watched the three bandits disappear without hesitation inside the bank.

Collecting the reins of the horses, Cole's eyebrow raised, and he shot a look of apprehension towards Clell, who acknowledged in return with his own conciliatory smile and a light tap of his hand on his LeMat.

Both men glanced nervous looks in all directions as they waited for the robbers to flee from the bank. They became restless as the seconds passed into minutes, and their adrenaline raced, increasing their body temperature.

Clell's face flushed and his legs became a little shaky. He bit hard on his pipe to control his quivers. He slanted an ear towards the bank on his left side and listened, but he heard nothing, so he twisted to look hard through the large glass window.

He could make out the figure of Jesse with his gun pointing at the cashier's window, but little else. However, he did notice the bank door was still slightly ajar, and he thought this looked inviting to passers-by.

He nodded his head and furrowed his brow in Cole's direction to indicate something wasn't right. He tapped out his pipe and casually walked over to the door to pull it secure. As he turned around from the door, a man approached and stood directly to his front, blocking his way.

The stranger had observed the suspicious behaviour of the two men from his hardware store across the thoroughfare, and he had decided to approach and investigate.

Both the men's eyes locked on each other, but Clell noticed the stranger cast a glance to the side of his shoulder and through the glass door.

The man's face betrayed his stern poise as he tried to conceal that he had seen Jesse throw the bank cashier to the floor. Clell immediately noticed the expression change and grabbed the man's lapel with his left hand as, at the same time, he pulled back his long duster to reveal his LeMat.

"Get the hell out of here and keep your God-damned mouth shut," he ordered, pushing the storekeeper from the boardwalk. "Now walk on. You hear me? Walk on and don't say a word."

Observing the incident from just a few yards away, nineteen-year-old Henry Wheeler's suspicions were also raised, and he instantly reacted by shouting, "They're robbing the bank!"

Clell turned at an angle and, facing Wheeler, he unholstered his LeMat and pointed the barrel in Wheeler's direction.

"Shut your God-damn mouth," he hollered, but ignoring the gunman, Wheeler turned and ran, shouting out the call again repeatedly as he fled. Clell fired off one shot deliberately above the young man's head and yelled at him again.

"Stop your hollering!"

Before the shot had finished echoing around the buildings in Northfield, both Wheeler and the man on the boardwalk had begun to flee, both crying out loudly, "Robbery! Robbery!… Get your guns, boys! They're robbing the bank!"

Clell ran back to the bank and, opening the door, he raged, "Come on quick. They're on to us." His face paled as before him he could see Jesse with his pistol pressed hard against a bearded man's neck.

"Open the God-damn safe," Jesse ordered, ignoring Clell.

To Jesse's side, Clell could see Bob with a knife held against another man, and beyond the counter, he could see Frank kneeling in the vault and turning the dial on the safe.

"It won't open," Clell heard Frank call out. "The darn thing won't open, Jesse!"

"Come on, Jesse. We've got to move… and now," Clell hollered again as behind him out on the street he heard guns roar.

He turned to see Cole mount his horse and begin to pull Jesse's, Bob's, and Frank's horses by the reins towards the bank doorway as all around him the citizens of Northfield had begun running in all directions.

Some were taking cover, but he could clearly make out some of the other less fearful men loading up their weapons.

"Come on, we've got the horses," he yelled again, glancing inside the bank.

Although his warning calls were loud, he knew Jesse was bedevilled and that his plea would be ignored.

"Open the safe!" Again Clell heard Jesse order in anger and frustration, and he froze as he saw Jesse hit the unresponsive man hard over the side of the head with his pistol, sending him crashing to the floor.

"I can't!" the terrified banker screamed as he stumbled up to his knees.

Jesse withdrew a pocket knife and crouched over the felled man with the blade pressed hard under his chin.

"Open it or I'll cut your damn throat from ear to ear, you God-damned son of a bitch."

Closing his eyes and drawing in a composing breath, the banker answered, "Then you'll have to cut my throat."

"Wh... at?" Jesse frowned, his eyes mantling disbelief as he applied more pressure with the blade until blood began to seep out and trickle onto the man's paper shirt collar.

"The safe has a chronometer fitted and it will not open." The banker lied, and Jesse reacted with natural violence by stoving in the cashier's head with the barrel of his pistol.

"Clell! Clell!" Cole shouted out from the street. "We've got to get the hell out of here and fast." A bullet hissed over Cole's head as he beckoned Clell to move and join him by waving his hand.

Clell's eyes flicked right and left. He could see something in the presence of the Northfield residents he had never encountered before.

They seemed ardent with an unfearing determination and grit to fight back and not to give up their hard-earned cash to the southern guerrillas.

Armed men were beginning to position themselves in doorways, and gun-wielding shadows were visible behind glass and on the terraces above.

His mouth became dry, and he slid his tongue along the inside of his lips to draw moisture as he gripped tight on the walnut handle of the LeMat.

Dan Goodall, a medical student from Chicago, had been on his way to the livery for a hired buggy when he heard the first shot. He and his fiancée, Hollie Cobb, had planned an afternoon picnic at Spring Creek, where he hoped the couple would confirm the final arrangements for their wedding later in the year.

Dan pushed Hollie forcefully into the safety of the lobby of the Dampier Hotel just as Henry Wheeler scrambled by.

"Get your guns. They're robbing the bank," Wheeler repeated as he fled up the stairs.

Without hesitation, Goodall grabbed an old army carbine which was leant against the brolly stand and checked the magazine for cartridges. He then, shrugged away the detaining arms of Hollie and ignored her calls for him not to get involved and stepped back outside into the bright afternoon sunlight on Division Street to look towards the First National Bank.

Bill Chadwell, Charlie Pitts, and Jim Younger had reacted to the gunshots by galloping across the bridge and towards the bank. With pistols drawn, they fired off repeated shots high into the sky and yelled out warnings for everyone to get off the street.

Cole and Clell noticed the actions of their guerrilla comrades, and so they too mounted and began to ride up and down Division Street discharging their weapons into the clear blue, hoping the violence would stamp out the locals' bravery and deter them from taking up arms.

Dan Goodall ignored the terror yells and the threats of death as he squinted down the barrel of the carbine and took aim at the leading charger.

Squeezing hard on the trigger, his head jolted back, but through the thick gun smoke, he was able to see that blood had burst out from the target's chest as the missile bore through flesh and bone.

The intense pain of the shot forced Bill to involuntarily stand from his saddle. He threw a bewildered smile at Goodall, then his neck went limp and his head dropped loosely forward. Falling sidewards from his horse, Bill was dead before he thudded against the hard, dry mud.

More shots were unleashed at the riders from all angles and locations as more of the angered menfolk of Northfield armed themselves and took to defending and protecting their wealth.

A man called Manning, who owned the gun store, ran out onto the street and stood at Goodall's side on the unprotected sidewalk to also begin discharging his breech-loading rifle at the horsemen.

Wheeler had reached his hotel room and was now armed with his rifle. As fast as he could, he repeatedly fired down from his room window at the charging pack.

Derringers, pistols, shotguns, and rifles were being fired relentlessly from the sidewalks, rooftops, windows, and doorways. Thick grey smoke began to hang low as chaos and shock mastered the outlaws' cogitations.

Leaving Bill in a swelling pool of blood, Jim and Charlie continued to charge up and down Division Street. With their heads hung low behind their horses, they repeatedly and randomly discharged their pistols into the sky and downwards into the dry, hard mud in an effort to clear the street of the vigilantes without injuring or killing anyone.

Clell pulled up outside the bank to beseech Jesse to flee once more. He dismounted, ran to the door, and looked through the glass pane.

"Come on Jesse! Now!" he shouted. "They've all turned on us."

This time, Clell could not hear what was being said from beyond the bank doors because of the deafening roar of gun discharge and the galloping of hooves, but he could clearly see the cold gaze of murder in Jesse's pale eyes.

"Get off the damn street!" Clell glanced over his shoulder to see Cole charging back towards the bank, yelling out to the increasing number of residents who were taking up arms against the bank robbers. He pulled his horse alongside a blonde-haired teenager who was standing outside Bierman's furniture store and repeated the call, but fear had numbed him and he did not move. "Hurry boys, they're shooting us to pieces!" Now Clell called out his plea to Frank and Bob, who reacted by knocking the second cashier to the floor as they scrambled towards the doorway.

Jesse held his poise and leered at his wounded prisoner, then he grinned and spun to make his exit, but upon reaching the doorway, he looked back and raised his Remington .44 and fired a solitary shot into the spasming man's temple. Blood and brains sprayed across the polished counter and wetted the open pages of the ledger.

Clell turned away from the bank, shaking his head towards the floorboards in reaction to the disgusting vision of sickening and needless murder. He jumped back into the saddle, but as he pulled on the reins, he was hit in the face by shotgun pellets, which thrust him back in the saddle.

He fought hard against the agony to stay mounted and hold on to the leather, but completely disoriented, and with a curtain of thick red hindering his vision, Clell screamed out as intense pain ravaged through his punctured left eye and shredded face.

His horse spun several times as he tried in vain to regain his stability. With blurred vision and scrambled senses, he was lost to the events surrounding him as he struggled in the pain-riveted wilderness.

Cole saw the blood spray out from Clell's face and he swerved his horse in the direction of the wounded man as he fired off repeated shots at Goodall and Manning.

Wood shattered above their heads and instinctively they both ducked and dropped to the floor as Cole passed them by to pull up his horse next to Clell.

"I've got ya Clell," he screamed as he leaned over and took hold of Clell's reins.

"Ride, damn it!" Cole heard Jesse shout as he and Frank both ignored Clell and thundered past him. Cole knew they were only interested in their own self-preservation.

"Ride or get buried," Frank shouted to Jim Younger, who had turned his horse to help Clell and pulled up alongside his brother, Cole.

"Come on Cole, let's get going before they plant us," Jim urged, randomly firing his pistol, but as he awaited his brother's reply, a bullet whistled past his face, taking with it a slice of his top lip. Driven by the immediate agony, Jim spurred his horse into a gallop and, with one hand screening the gruesome flapping wound, he followed on fast behind Frank and Jesse away from the bridge and towards the opposite end of the town.

Cole began to turn and lead Clell's horse. In the chaos he had dropped his pistol, but Clell, with his head drooping and gritted teeth, had gripped hard on his LeMat and continued to blindly shoot off bullets.

"For God's sake, don't leave me!" Clell heard the call from Cole's younger brother, Bob. "Some low-down son of a bitch has killed my horse." He felt Cole spin the horses in the direction of the plea.

Bob's horse had been deliberately shot by Henry Wheeler, who had been shooting down at the robbers from his hotel window as they fled from the bank. To save himself, Bob had to scurry along the boardwalk and dive for cover under the open-air stairwell of Lee and Hitchcock's dry goods store, where he pressed himself tight against the brick wall and out of sight of the shooting Wheeler above. He managed to return fire on Wheeler and, for a brief moment, the gunfire intensified as the pair of shootists became locked in their own duel to the death.

Again Clell heard Bob yell out, only this time he screamed out in pain as his elbow had been shattered by a bullet from above. That was the last sound Clell Miller ever heard, as Dan Goodall had taken another timed and precise aim at the stranded figure twenty yards away and squeezed upon his trigger to release a perfectly targeted bullet into the shoulder of the LeMat-wielding outlaw. The blast tore deep through flesh and knocked Clell out of the saddle to land face first into the solid dirt. With a bone-cracking thud, he expelled his last breath, and he released the LeMat from his grip to spin loose on the street.

Chapter 6

September 7th, 1876.

Six minutes after the James-Younger gang rode into Northfield, Nicholas Gustavson was still unable to move and obey Cole's repeated warnings to get off the street.

His body was locked rigid with fear as he watched the death scene unfold in front of him. Gun smoke had burned his eyes as he watched Cole frantically trying to turn and lead on the panicked horses, and he saw the back of Clell's body burst open and splatter blood high in all directions.

He was still motionless seconds later when he saw Clell's bloodied body drop dead to the floor, and he remained in the same rigid position with his eyes following Cole as he frantically galloped past him again, as the outlaw this time tried to make a desperate dash for freedom.

Nicholas's scared body remained set with his legs and feet locked in position until suddenly his eyes caught a glimpse through the smog of the discarded and still-spinning LeMat at the side of Clell's dead body.

Just seconds after the wind from Cole's galloping horse had ruffled his blonde hair, Nicholas sped forward, ignoring the whistling bullets that were heading in Cole's direction from Goodall and Manning. He dived down to clasp both his hands around Clell's abandoned LeMat.

Crouching on his knees, he cradled the LeMat in his hands and, lowering his head and opening his eyes wider, he gaped at the ornate killing machine.

He was now deaf to the sounds of gunfire, and he did not hear the yells from Goodall and Manning urging him to get out of the way, nor did he see Cole spin around on his horse and charge to the rescue of his wounded brother Bob, who was still sheltering under the staircase.

Young Nicholas was completely oblivious to the bone-crushing impact from Cole's horse, which killed him instantly, as bullets from Goodall and Manning had ripped deep into Cole's hip and right arm, causing him to drop the reins and momentarily lose control of his mount at full gallop. The gelding veered to the right and collided with Nicholas, tossing him high from the ground and flipping him over onto his back.

Expelling his last breath with gasping pain and a mouthful of blood, Nicholas's shattered body lay on its back with his watery eyes fixed skywards.

Levi Clayton was close enough to clearly hear the gut-sickening crunch of bone smashing against bone as he watched, from his unrestricted view, young Nicholas's body being tossed high.

Clayton had been cautiously observing the events unfurl from the shadow of Holmberg's barber shop doorway with his gun drawn and ready to fire, but the Englishman had deemed it unnecessary to involve himself in the fracas outside the bank.

He had been in America long enough to witness wanton murder and merciless slaughter of innocent bystanders on too many occasions, and he considered it wise to be discreet when guns started blazing and lives became endangered.

He had watched unaffected as the scene of death played out in front of him, and he remained unmoved when Cole, just a few yards away, hauled up his fellow outlaw brother from under the stairwell and sped off toward the bridge with bullets hailing all about them.

Still, Levi remained unmoved when he saw a now excitable Goodall, Manning, and a few others following the hoofprints and blood trail to give chase to the fleeing wounded outlaws.

Now fully out of ammunition, the excitable chasers continued hurling stones and rocks toward the lingering dust as Levi watched on, remaining calm and unmoved.

Heavy acrid smoke hung in the now eerie silence as the shocked citizens of Northfield began to populate the bloodied streets again. The wooden boardwalks creaked as they took very small and nervous steps out into the stillness.

Dazed and confused, their distressed eyes scanned across the bullet-ridden buildings, smashed windows, the three bloodied bodies, and a motionless horse.

Hollie Cobb broke from the pack and ran towards her uninjured fiancé to lock her arms tightly around his shoulders.

Breathing hard, only his gun-smoked face indicated Goodall had been involved in a bloody shootout.

Finally, and slowly, words began to be quietly exchanged. "Oh my Lord, look at all that blood." The noise and conversations gently increased until someone shouted out from the doorway of the First National that Lee Haywood had been murdered.

Levi Clayton did not join the mass as they hesitantly wandered between the bodies of Clell Miller, Charlie Pitts, and young Nicholas Gustavson. He looked down at the ghostly face of Clell from his fixed position in the shadows. He had no need to move closer to the bloodied bodies. He could clearly see Clell's greying eyes were fixed wide open with the all-too-familiar brace of death.

Across the street and through the statuette figures of the gathering, he looked at Gustavson's twisted body as it was being tentatively prodded by a teary elderly woman until suddenly his attention was drawn to a small shimmering object not less than ten yards away.

Squinting in the afternoon sun, Levi's eyes inquisitively settled upon the reflection in the dust. There at the edge of the sidewalk, and not seen by anyone other than himself, discarded in the dusty soil, was the maligned LeMat.

Euphoria gradually descended upon the men and women of Northfield as the realisation of their heroics began to unfold.

Goodall and Manning were momentarily raised high onto shoulders and paraded through the town like heroes, but the spectacle soon ended when Goodall began to shout that a posse should be formed to give chase, and so within minutes, the clamour began to rearm, mount, and pursue the fleeing wounded bandits.

Chapter 7

October 15th, 1876.

Levi Clayton stretched out his aching limbs as the railroad carriage pulled to an ear-grating halt in Black Hawk. Almost fourteen years had passed since Levi had last stood in the dreary streets of Black Hawk.

The former gold mining town looked almost unrecognisable in the low afternoon sun to the traveller as he peered through the glass and along the orderly rows of brick buildings, which had long since replaced the scattering of timber-framed, log-built shanties to which he once had been accustomed.

With the completion of a business transaction in Northfield accomplished, Levi had decided to return to Black Hawk and attend to an obligation that had plagued his mind for many years.

During his previous six-month stay in the hellhole of Black Hawk, Levi hadn't become acquainted with many people. He reminisced about his friend Doc McCurdy, who had been slain without mercy as a result of his own naïve misjudgments. He recalled the tall and steely Sheriff who kept him under lock and key for five of the six months, and he fondly brought to mind the alluring face of Molly, the gratifying lady of the night.

He fondly recollected the aroma of her strong, zesty perfume and her youthful energy, but as the train door opened, sulphur pierced his nostrils, and the pleasurable memory was replaced with his final vision of her pox-riddled body decaying in a darkened room.

Arising from the chair, he shuddered and banished the repulsive ghost of Molly, and he reached up for his case to disembark the train through the low-hanging discharge of steam.

The town was almost beyond recognition to Levi. The street layout was the same, but both the buildings and the congestion of milling people appeared to have doubled in number.

Gold miners were replaced by foundry workers, and the line of horse-drawn coaches had been replaced by the iron-tracked station house.

Levi ambled down Main Street. The Long Horn Hotel was still clearly visible, but it was now a four-storey bulk. The Dark Star Saloon had been replaced with another hotel, and Morgan's Tub and Scrub was now an engineering office. Levi decided to adventure a little further before checking into his hotel, all the time reminiscing and retracing his former steps in Black Hawk.

Molly's cabin had been overlaid, but to his right was the same fetid log cabin that he had occupied for almost six months of his life.

Looking almost exactly the same as when he left it, the Sheriff's office and jail occupied a regal and elevated position on a newly constructed four-way junction.

There was no mistake. Levi looked at the same notice board he had seen fourteen years earlier. He recalled the wanted poster for Charlie Brownsword and the resulting fallout over the bounty money with his friend, the 'Doc'.

Now the notices displayed higher-value rewards for Jesse James and the Cole Younger gang. He released a wry smile, wondering if the posse back in Northfield had caught up with their prey, but his thoughts were soon again propelled to the present as the unmistakable sound of boots approaching on the wooden boardwalk behind him diverted his gaze.

"Aft'noon," greeted the tall silver-bearded man as he tipped his hat.

"Hello, Sheriff," Levi replied, as his eyes levelled with Black Hawk's lawman.

"Got something you want to tell me, Mister?" the Sheriff asked.

Levi paused for a moment, his hand gripping the handle of the LeMat under his jacket. The Sheriff, who stood three feet away from him, was Sheriff Kelton—the same man who locked him up for almost six months all those years ago. There was no mistake.

Although now in his late fifties and his face shadowed by the high sun, his features were still clearly recognisable.

The same stern countenance was present on the sharp, angular features, and his middle-aged skin was still stretched tight across his high cheekbones, but now his thick black hair had long since drained of its colour, leaving it with a lustre of pure silver.

"I'm thinking you're going to be in need of a new poster, Sheriff." Levi apprehensively smiled, wondering if the Sheriff would recognise him. He pulled the brim of his hat lower as if to shade his eyes from the sun's bright rays, which cut through the peaks of the mountains behind the Sheriff's broad shoulders.

"Oh, yeah?" The Sheriff's eyes narrowed after hearing the hint of unfamiliar English tones. "And how do you figure that, stranger?" he asked, intensifying his glare on the exclusively clad foreigner, knowing he had a concealed hand carefully on his pistol.

"I've just travelled down from Northfield, Minnesota, where I saw the townsfolk there just about annihilate this here James gang." Levi pointed with his thumb over his shoulder and in the direction of the wanted poster. He felt the need to cut the conversation and move on, fearing the longer he held the discussion the more it would increase the Sheriff's power of recall.

"That so, uh?" Sheriff Kelton paused. The man who stood before him had a curious familiarity about him. "I ain't read any reports stating or confirming such."

"Well, sir, I assure you, sir, I saw the whole darn thing myself, and it wasn't too pleasant either."

Now the Sheriff was almost certain he had met the younger man somewhere before, but with most of the outsider's face shadowed he was only able to see clearly his mouth and jawline, and he could not recall the familiarity nor confirm his suspicions.

"You saw them bring down Jesse James and Cole Younger?" His voice embodied doubt.

"Not exactly." Levi took an unconscious small step backwards. "But I did see the whole gang get shot up pretty bad, and two of them shot outright dead not more than ten feet in front of me."

The Sheriff's intuition told him the stranger was telling the truth, and he held the brief silence, indicating that he wanted more.

"Then when I was on my way over here from Northfield, I read that they had busted up the Younger brothers and hauled them in. Papers said all three are near to dead, and that it's only a matter of days before Jesse and Frank James are apprehended."

"And just what in the darnation are the James boys doing that far north?" Kelton thought out loud, a scratch on his chin accompanying his perplexity.

"I'm not sure about that. I'm not from around these parts. All I know is that they were trying to rob the bank in Northfield and it all went terribly wrong for them." Levi removed his hand from within his jacket in an effort to eliminate the notable suspicion, but he knew the veteran had noted the weapon.

"Northfield, you say. Mighty long distance you've travelled." The Sheriff's comment was a question for which he expected a reply.

"Yes, sir. Got a little business to finish." Levi knew it was in a Sheriff's nature to be inquisitive, but he feared this Sheriff's interest was beyond routine.

"That so?" Again Sheriff Kelton tried to angle a look at the stranger's obscured face. "Business here in Black Hawk?"

"Yes, sir. Something I should have done a long time ago," Levi answered honestly.

"Business I need to know about?" Kelton raised his eyebrows as he spoke.

"Not at all, Sheriff... just a personal obligation."

"Kelton. My name is Sheriff Kelton." He held out his hand to offer a formal introduction. "Maybe you'd like to get a bit of the sun off your shoulders and come inside a while." Kelton twisted the palm of his hand toward the office door. "And you can tell me all about this darn robbery."

"I'm afraid I'm right pressed for time just now, Sheriff." Levi noted the sudden change in Kelton's face as he began to decline the invite. His friendly smile had dropped away to reveal a disapproving scowl.

"Well, maybe you could drop by a little later when times are a little less pressing." There was more than a hint of discontentment in the Sheriff's suggestion. "Then you can tell me more about the shoot-up at your leisure."

"It will be my pleasure, Sheriff." Levi tipped his hat with one finger and stepped aside.

"Remind me, what did you say your name was?" Now the Sheriff was convinced he had encountered the man before.

"Good day, Sheriff." Levi ignored the query and simply nodded without looking back. He moved past the Sheriff and walked down the steps and out onto the dry mud street.

"Well, okay then." Kelton released a wary smile and muttered to himself, "I'll be seeing you around, stranger."

He then watched Levi gradually drop out of sight before finally entering his office. Dropping heavily into his well-worn leather chair, he swung his legs onto his desk and then poured out a coffee. He took to interrogating his recollections.

Levi did not look back; he resisted the urge. He was sure the scrutinising eyes of the Sheriff would be upon him. Instead, he advanced at pace until he disappeared from view in the rapidly descending dullness, due to the sun dropping quickly behind the mountains.

He knew the Sheriff had seen him place his hand on the LeMat and that it was a mistake.

He hoped he had not provoked the Sheriff's mistrust or aroused any long-abandoned memories. He wanted to complete his affairs in Black Hawk quickly and without trouble.

Comfortable but not at ease in the modest Long Horn Hotel, the encounter with the Sheriff had baited Levi with painful, distant memories which, until now, he had repressed from his thoughts.

Laid on the bed, he toyed with the LeMat as his mind flooded back to fourteen years ago when he was jailed for a murder he did not commit. He did not blame the Sheriff for his actions. He surmised he was only doing his job, but the pain of that fateful night when he was shot and then accused of killing his best friend had been ignited within him.

Almost six months he languished in Black Hawk's jail in a deathly state and was only cared for by an insane war veteran.

The memories were not pleasant, and he concluded, as he closed his eyes to rest, that the quicker he completed his business in Black Hawk, the better.

A good rest in the comfortable bed was much needed and welcomed after the lengthy journey into Black Hawk, and now fully refreshed with his belly filled, Levi again ventured out into the streets.

This time he did not retrace any of his former steps; he followed the route given to him by the hotel manager. "'A little early for chasing ghosts,'" the manager quipped, hoping the remark would lead to a response from the stranger which would indicate why he wanted to visit the cemetery.

Without reply or acknowledgement, Levi followed the track out of town and away from the smells of the mills and foundries. He continued for almost an hour following the manager's route, passing through forested inclines until he reached a large grassy opening on the hillside, which was studded with an array of grave markers.

Fresh pine now filled his nostrils instead of sulphur and iron, and led the way to a rudimentary sign on the gatepost that read 'Funerary Garden'.

Levi scanned across the peaceful sloping field and sighed as lamented sentiments took away his breath. He paused a while before moving on, as the early morning sun had not lifted the grey mist from the realm of the dead, and all was eerily silent.

In this field, he hoped to find the graves of his friends Doc McCurdy and Martha 'Molly' Lytle.

The stiffness of the gate and the length of the undisturbed grass indicated that not many people ventured out this far from town anymore. The screeching of the hinges broke the silence and provoked the resting birds to rise and flee from the long grass. For another long moment, he paused, looking left, right, then ahead at the array of wooden markers, plaques, headstones, simple wooden crosses, and decorated carvings made from tree trunks.

The thought that he could have been planted and left to rot in this field with an unmarked grave crossed his mind. He paused a while, but he was determined that his friend's memory should be commemorated if possible, and so, with another shudder, he moved on.

Etched on the wood, granite, and marble were the last remembrances of those who were now resting in eternal peace.Florence Pendleton died 1867, J. N. Hyder died 1863, Susanna Hoops died 1862, Edwin Langdon died 1861.

The names of the murdered, the diseased, the exhausted, the premature, the infected, the accidental went on and on, but Levi ignored the ornate stone and granite epitaphs. He knew no one would have grieved enough to honour McCurdy and Molly with a costly memorial, and after another thirty minutes of ghoulish curiosity, he stopped at a simple rotten plank which stated McCurdy 1861.

He dropped his head, closed his eyes, and quietly and flawlessly recited the words from Charles Garthwords: 'Heavenly Father I call upon ye'.

Levi devoted another two hours or so searching for Molly's grave, but he always knew that no one in Black Hawk would care for a whore once she was no longer desirable, and as expected no memorial could be found.

Levi Clayton's business in Black Hawk was now accomplished and the following morning he was booked on the Overland to Denver, where he planned to board the train to his adopted hometown of Placerville, California.

Earlier, he had visited the stone carvers in nearby Central City and made a payment for a deserving grave marker, one of distinction for Doctor Fergus McCurdy, a man he hadn't known for long and a man flawed but a man he would be forever indebted to.

Darkness descended early and fast upon the town in the valley, and the Englishman had decided to pass his final night with a nostalgic visit to Van De Lyden's Saloon.

With his mind flooded with reminiscences of the past, he drew in a breath of the cool night air and gazed upwards to the stars, which resembled diamonds scattered on a dark velvet cloth. They glistened and flickered against the black cloudless sky high above Black Hawk. He stood out of view from anyone in the blackness opposite the brick new merchants store which had replaced Molly's cabin.

He felt unsatisfied because he had not managed to locate her resting place and erect a memorial which she deserved, and his conscience allowed his mind to flood with the reminiscences he had struggled for years to banish.

He watched his past shadow cross the street and approach the blurry vision of the small wooden cabin exactly as he did fourteen years earlier.

The building was in total darkness and he recalled wondering if she was there. He pressed his ear against the side of the cabin—maybe she was entertaining. No, the cabin lay in total silence. Maybe she was out trying to attract a punter in one of the saloons, or maybe she had died just as the Sheriff had insinuated.

With a burning desire to seek out the truth of what had happened to his friend, McCurdy pressed Levi on towards the door. He recollected every moment, and he watched himself from across the street.

He remained motionless as he saw himself wait at Molly's door and listen momentarily, then he gazed all around him, but he remembered only the silence and blackness.

He slowly turned the door handle, and to his surprise, the door opened. Quickly and silently, he stepped inside, but he drew to a halt before he fully entered the room. Someone was lying on the bed sleeping. He listened without moving any further. It was at that moment his nostrils were assaulted with a repulsive stench, and his stomach churned from the vile smell of rotting flesh.

The memory was now clear, and he recalled every morbid detail. He had clasped his hand over his nose and mouth and bungled his way backward out of the door.

"Who's there?" The almost inaudible whisper was repeated until Levi, who was arched over replenishing his lungs with the fresh night air, heard the call from within.

Leaving the door open to let in much-needed fresh night air and replacing his hand over his mouth, Levi returned inside the one-room building. He did not speak as he slowly approached the bed.

The room was freezing cold and his breath clouded in front of him.

"Is someone there?" The faint croaky voice, which was unrecognisable, was that of Molly. He shuddered at the sound of her pain, which he had put out of his mind for over fourteen years until now. Gone were her usual soft, seductive tones.

"Please help me," she faintly pleaded.

Levi could just make out the bulk of her body in the bed, and once again he fought to compose himself as the perfidious rotting stench wrenched at his stomach. He remained silent, not daring to remove his covering hand from his nose, as he fumbled and failed to light a bedside lantern.

As the foulness smarted his eyes, the harrowing shock bestowed upon them stunned him.

A skeletal Molly occupied the bed. Only her face and one dangling arm were visible. She looked dead. Dozens of flies were foraging on her deathly pale skin, whilst masses of maggots chewed away at the folds of loose flesh in the joints of her exposed arm and hand.

Again Levi was forced to compose himself and, trying for a second time, he managed to light the lantern bright enough to allow its orange glow to illuminate his face.

Molly's eyes enlarged slightly, revealing her surprise. Her lips cracked open, and she released a whisper.

"Lordy, I'm in heaven." The linen where she lay was soiled and crusted with dry sweat.

"I'm afraid not," Levi confirmed. "Not yet."

"Then have you come to take me over to the other side?" she begged, trembling.

"No, I'm afraid I haven't come for that either." The strong reek of decay combined with the sight of the near-corpse forced Levi to step back.

"Well then, why has a ghost come to visit me? Have you come to ask me to repent my sins before I finally die?" she wondered.

"I'm sorry, Molly, but I'm not a ghost. It's me, Levi... Levi Clayton. The Englishman. Do you remember me?"

"Well, sure I do." Her throat was dry. The words were feeble and hard for Levi to hear, and he had to bend lower to angle his ear towards the sound.

"I might be losing my fight for life, Levi, but my mind ain't completely defunct. Not yet, anyhow."

Levi had to recoil from the putrescent smell of decaying flesh.

Even now, after all the passing years, he could recall every word, every smell, and the suffering that had clasped its vice upon Molly.

"I know it's you, Levi, but after Bartlett shot you, the Sheriff told me you'd be lucky to make it through the night. The last thing I heard was that you were knocking on death's door... waiting for it to open. I thought you'd be well gone by now." The effort of speaking was too much for Molly, and she coughed violently until a release of black bile rose from her throat, which she ejected onto her shoulder. Levi clenched hard on his teeth as he remembered Molly mentioning the name of Bartlett.

He held his breath and recomposed himself to draw near to her again, then he poured out some stale water from a bedside jug into a bowl.

"I guess the Sheriff underestimated my resistance." He dipped a cloth into the bowl and then, being careful not to disturb the bed linen in fear of the odours it might release, he wiped Molly's face.

Although her skin was as pale as the mountain snow, her brow was burning, and Levi spliced the cloth, enabling him to leave one damp half on her forehead as he brushed away from her skin the flies and their encrusted eggs.

"I'm glad you survived, Levi. You're a rare kind of man, and you didn't deserve to die in this …" Her voice wore out, and her last words fell silent.

Levi smelt and examined the water, but it smelt fetid, and dead flies were floating on its cloudy surface.

He glanced around for another form of tonic, and he saw on a cabinet to the side of the room a small bottle of whisky.

Carefully he held the bottleneck to her lips, just enough to allow a couple of droplets to fall onto her tongue. She responded by smacking her lips to indicate more, and then she continued.

"But you've shattered my hopes, Levi. I've been laid here in this darkness so long waiting to die that I figured the next light I saw would be the glow from a halo. Then when I saw your face in front of me I thought, 'Jesus Christ, thank the Lord, I must be dead,' and all the pain vanished."

Her mouth and jaw seemed to become taut, and Levi dripped in a few more droplets of the alcohol.

"Now I know I'm alive and it still hurts like hell. Help me die, Levi, please stop the pain. Please help me die." She tried in vain to raise her hand towards him. "I'm begging you."

"I can't do that, Molly." Levi shook his head. "God will call you when it's your time, but before he does, you must tell me what happened to Doctor McCurdy." Again he lubricated her dry throat with more beads of whisky. "Can you do that, Molly, for me? Can you please remember what happened to my friend, the Doc?"

Her eyes rolled back, and she fought for every breath as though it were her last. "He ain't been around here. Nobody ain't been to see me… except you."

She faltered and fell silent. Levi refreshed the cloth on her forehead, and she strained to respond.

"You see, when you've got a sexy figure, a warm smile, and you're prepared to do favours, they all come a-flocking, wanting to get to know you real well. But when you take all that away and you feel kinda woozy, no one comes anywhere near." Levi interrupted, fearing she may pass away at any moment.

"I know he hasn't been here to see you. He's dead. Someone killed him and I need to know who." Confused, she frowned and her eyes rolled over white. Levi saw that she was ailing fast.

"Molly. Listen to me. It's very important. Doc McCurdy was with you the night Bartlett shot me. Sometime later, he was killed and I need to know why and who killed him."

"No… no… no, I can't remember. It was so long ago."

"You must try, Molly. Please try to remember." Again, more droplets were released into Molly's mouth.

"Think, Molly. Please think back to that night in Van De Lyden's."

"I can't. It was such a……" Levi saw her eyes rolling over again and her eyelids flicker slowly.

"Molly! You must. God won't let you die until you tell me what happened to McCurdy." Levi was desperate for an answer and any indication of a clue.

She went silent, and her raspy breath shallowed as she began to drift into unconsciousness. Levi stimulated her again with more whisky, which provoked a shudder and an almost inaudible response.

"You think that God will call me?"

"Sure I do. He's keeping you alive until you can recall what happened."

"Oh. The doctor, oh yes. I remember. I can remember him now, cards and booze. I recall him now. That drunkard McCurdy. But will you do me one last favour?"

"Yes, of course. Anything." Levi agreed with urgency.

Molly seemed temporarily reinvigorated, and she managed to pull from under the linen her other hand, in which she clutched her Bible.

Levi was forced to hold his breath again and step back as a new release of putrid vapours filled the room.

"Levi, I want you to swear on the Holy Bible. Will you do as I beg?"

"I swear." He impatiently reached out and tentatively touched the Bible's worn leather cover with his fingers. It was damp and warm from her body perspiration.

"I have all my life's savings under my pillow. I want you to take it to Boyle County, Kentucky, and give it to Nora Hood in Danville. She is my sister, and she's looking after my son, Nathaniel. She is the town's schoolteacher, so you should easily find her. I've been meaning to write, but..."

Levi recalled he had to press her at this point for a response. He had just escaped the noose and he was anxious to leave town quickly with the answer he needed to hear.

"Molly, what about Doc McCurdy?"

"Yes... yes... yes, let me finish and I'll tell you all about the Doc," she stammered.

"Leave me enough for a decent funeral and take out what you need for your expenses and give the rest to her for Nathaniel's upkeeping." Although contorted with pain, she turned slightly to put her hand under the pillow.

"There is just one more thing."

"Yes?" he replied calmly, but he desperately wanted her to hurry. *Come on, for Christ's sake. No wonder you're taking so long to die if you drag things out as long as this,* he griped silently.

"My name is not Molly. It is Martha, Martha Lytle, and Nora believes that I work in a bank. Please don't let her think any different, will you?"

"No, but…"

"You will have to make up something about my death. Don't let her know I died like this. Can you fulfil this dying wish for me, Levi?"

"Of course I can, and I will… I promise. But now please tell me what you know about Doctor McCurdy's death."

"Oh, I remember that night well. It had been a bad night for me. I had hoped you would come back for more comfort, but you didn't show. There was no business at all that night anywhere and I hadn't earned a cent.

In fact I'd given up all hope of any trade and I was just leaving the Dark Star when the Doc showed some interest in me." She paused to cough more phlegm into her hand repeatedly.

"He called me over. I knew he was drunk and well past it, but I thought what the hell, it's easy money for nothing. I remember asking him for the money upfront because I didn't want him to think I was free and besides, the drunks never want to pay afterward. When he felt inside his jacket for his wallet, he began to panic. He went berserk, claiming it had been stolen."

Each time she began to utter words with a fresh intake of breath, but by the time she had neared the end of her sentence she struggled to make her voice heard and her words slowed until they were omitted in a hoarse slur.

"At first he accused me of lifting his money, but then, in a fuming rage, he dragged me along with him to Van De Lyden's to confront you. He was darn near flabbergasted when he saw you gaming against Bartlett. One minute he'd be saying you were a total fool and the next he'd be admiring you. We were both shocked right through to our bones when we saw you pull your gun on Bartlett and call him a cheat. I guess it was because we knew Bartlett would worm his way out of it somehow, but we did not for any moment consider how.

The Doc was devastated when he saw you get gunned down and straight away he threatened to have Bartlett run into jail. All the while, the cowards who saw the shooting began fearing reprisals from Bartlett and his hired hands, so they agreed to back Bartlett by making a pact and saying that he acted in self-defence. All hell let loose and Doctor McCurdy flew at Bartlett with his fists, but he was knocked down by one of Bartlett's men and when he got up again, he had your gun in his hand. It all happened in a flash. At first you were laying there in a pool of blood and then just minutes later so was Doctor McCurdy. I couldn't believe it."

"Is that it all?"

"Yes. It was all over so fast and you both disappeared without any trace, as if you'd never even been into Black Hawk."

"Well," Levi shook his head. "Who pulled the trigger? Was it Bartlett?"

"It surely was. The scumbag didn't give the Doc a chance. One bullet straight, plumb through his head without warning." She paused momentarily to beat her tongue about her mouth in a bid to lubricate her dry throat, and again Levi responded by aiding her with more droplets of whisky.

"Felled him without any mercy," she angrily added.

"Didn't you do anything?" It was just an instantaneous comment from Levi. He knew that she would not have been alive if she had tried to intervene.

"What could I do, Levi?" she gulped hard.

"I gave a statement to the Sheriff, and he just tossed it in his drawer, saying, 'Who the hell is going to believe the words of a woman who sells her body against that of all those testifiers?'

Bartlett had got it all figured out and squared away before the Sheriff even got in there."

"That cowardly bastard!" Levi had been full of hateful revenge; he wanted to go out into the street and be able to look Bartlett in the eye and bring him to justice, but he knew that this was impossible and that his time with Molly had expired.

He looked down at her as she lay silent, and his mind thought of McCurdy and his now fatherless son. *Poor old soul did not deserve to die like that.* McCurdy had stretched his patience to the limits many times, but even with all of his faults he had become a friend, a true friend, and Levi now felt responsible for his death.

He vowed vengeance, but now, gratified by the information Molly had given him, he felt anxious. He turned the palm of his hand onto the woman's clammy cheek and said,

"Molly, I'm sorry, but I've got to go now. There are people out there looking for me." To his surprise, she slightly rallied again.

"Have you broken out of jail?"

"No, but I haven't got time to explain." With difficulty, he tried to prise himself away from her bedside, but he found it tough. He could not leave her to fester alone in her bed until she died.

"I'll find the druggist and pay him enough to come in and look after you." It was the best conclusion he could think of. The offer stirred Molly, and she raised her head from the pillow to reply.

"Pay him? Funny how money rules this town. That old fart toad once had to pay to come and see me." She paused to draw breath, which immediately caused her to cough once more. "No, no, no. Lev, don't bother wasting that hard-earned money on me now. I'm already as good as dead right now. Just take out enough to lay me deep and get over to Danville, then give the rest to my sister. Now, please go, I'm begging you. Please do as I ask."

"I've given you my word, Molly... err, Martha." Levi slowly backed away to the door. He was silent, stunned, and too saddened to speak any more, but just before he left he heard Molly try to raise her voice once again.

"T... th... ther... there is just one more thing, Levi. Don't you worry about ending up like me? I caught this misery long after I thought you were a goner."

He remembered remaining silently trapped with his thoughts of wasted lives as he turned out the night light and began to leave the room for the final time.

He slanted his head and turned his ear towards the bed as he heard Molly grumble under her breath.

"That God damn bitch of a preacher man."

The long wheeze of her last intake of breath caused Levi to stop at the door for one last glance back in the darkness as he tried to make out her motionless bulk in the bed. He became transfixed to the spot. *She's gone.* The thought slashed through his mind like a razor and split his reasoning.

The question crossed his mind as to what he should do next. *Go back and help? But if he did, what could he do? Or should he just get out of there fast?* He'd already been gone too long, and he again paused to stare at her body with his mind locked in this dilemma.

She moved. Yes, he was positive she had moved. Momentary relief engulfed him as he saw that she was still breathing... or was she? Maybe it had been the darkness playing tricks upon his strained eyes, or even possibly his mind was now hallucinating after suffering from months of pain and tedium that had been abruptly shattered by the unforeseen events of this long and far-from-overnight ordeal.

With his mind back in the present, he did not waste any more time thinking how he had enacted his revenge upon Bartlett or dwelling on the haunted past. He stepped out from the darkness and into the early descending dusk of the mountain county and headed towards the saloon.

No longer called Van De Lyden's, at first appearance the ownership appeared to be the only visible change, and the small wooden cabin seemed to be stuck in an era long past.

He swung past the double doors and leaned on the bar exactly as he did over a decade ago. As then, many stray bullets had slammed into the timber frame and had pierced through the aged, rotting wooden ceiling, which allowed shafts of light from the low moon to pierce cold rays through the dull cloud of thick cigar smoke and illuminate the overcrowding with a silverish glow.

Trade was brisk within the saloon; men stood shoulder to shoulder with each other, many of them revelling in intoxication, their conversations fused into an inaudible din.

Levi pushed his way through to the crude bar and ordered himself a bottle of the local blend, then half-leaning and twisting, he scanned across the bustle.

For a moment, his mind began to play tricks with him, as he felt Molly brush past his side, leaving in the air her unmistakable and unsubtle perfume to replace the barbaric stench of the liquor guzzlers.

Suddenly, a commotion erupted and Molly's presence vanished amongst the scrambling bodies.

"You're a cheating bastard, Doc Holliday!"

The revellers stumbled back to form a semicircle around the centre of the disruption, and silence replaced the drunken hum.

All eyes were fixed upon three seated gamblers and an angry-looking man who had risen with haste to his feet with his pistol drawn, knocking over his stool.

"Why, that is mighty rude of you, Mister Creech," calmly replied the gambler seated opposite the gun-brandishing man.

"You're a liar and a cheat, Holliday," spittle sprayed, "and I want my money back!" Although swaying and slurring his words, the man held firm his pointed pistol at his antagonist, John 'Doc' Holliday.

Remaining unconcerned that his life was at risk, Holliday nonchalantly gathered the notes and coins into the centre of the table, then scooped them up as he replied.

"Well, calm yourself, sir. Sit down and pick up your cards and get to winning it back."

"You take me for a fool, Holliday," he raged.

No one within the room moved, spoke, or tried to interact. The onlookers were accustomed to these types of arguments, and impending looks of doom were quickly branded on their suspended faces as they fully expected bloodshed and death.

"I ain't gonna allow you to cheat me or anyone else ever again," the gunman continued.

"Imperious and disturbing accusations you are making there, Mister Creech," Holliday smiled and held his gaze direct, but as he spoke he was unable to prevent a rattling cough.

"Why, you cocky son of a bitch," Creech bellowed, "get to your feet and defend yourself like a man."

Holliday ignored the order, and he began to pile up the array of silver coins, bearing a huge, satisfied grin.

"Draw!" Creech showed his rotten teeth and his chest inflated.

"You are embarrassing yourself," Holliday still calmly defied Creech's demands.

The mob wanted to see bloodshed, but the seated gambler wasn't one of them. He was an outsider with a peculiar, calculated demeanour.

He was younger than most in the room, and his skin was smooth and as pale as buttermilk.

He was immaculately dressed in expensive metropolitan attire, and his hands were free of industrious grime and calluses. He was the composed opposite of the bloodthirsty congregation.

"Get up and draw, damn it," Creech demanded.

"You are an embarrassment, Mister Creech, to your friends, and you are an embarrassment to this town." Holliday had now created three columns of silver eagles. "Now sit yourself, sir."

"Get up, Holliday, or I'll shoot you where you sit," Creech began to tense his finger on the trigger, and he held his arm steady. "I won't warn you again, Holliday. Now get up and draw your shooter!"

"Just look at you, a big brave rooster, Mister Creech. Standing there all menacingly bold and threatening me with your iron." Holliday's tone and words were clear, controlled, and stoically calm. "When I know you are nothing but a big clucking chicken." He finished organising the collection of coins and placed the palm of his right hand on the table, and still with his eyes locked in front of him, he allowed his left hand to clip open his jacket.

"Damn you, Holliday. Draw... draw now, you son of a bitch." Creech scowled hatred at Holliday.

"I advise you, sir, that if I stand you shall fall." As Holliday spoke, he held the assured stare.

Creech's pistol hammer rose, his mouth slanted, and extra lines appeared around his narrowing eyes.

Only Holliday foresaw Sheriff Kelton's timely intervention, but everyone heard the crack of steel against bone and the thud of Creech's unconscious body hitting the timber floor as Kelton's pistol whipped Creech across the back of his head.

"Obliged to you, Sheriff, for today you have saved me the cost of a funeral," Holliday smiled.

"Knock it off, Holliday." Sheriff Kelton did not welcome the boast. He had no time for outsiders, especially ones like Holliday who came into town to make a quick buck, then turned to making trouble when things went wrong. Although the life-threatening years of governing Black Hawk had not sapped his vigour, these gamblers and cold-blooded murderers turned the pit of his stomach. He had seen the likes of many Hollidays in the towns he had regulated, and his patience had long since departed from his skill set.

"Any more trouble and I'll be locking you up along with this fool," Kelton threatened.

"I guess I'm just a honey pot, Sheriff," Holliday held his smile, "that attracts all the wasps."

Shaking his head, Kelton chose to ignore the gambler, and he nudged Creech's body with the toe of his boot to see if he was still breathing.

Upon hearing an uncontrolled release and an intake of air, Kelton leant over Creech and slid both his hands under his shoulders, then he shouted out to the nearest of the onlookers.

"Come on, you loafers. Grab his feet and help me get him out of here."

As Kelton and a few of the others dragged the unconscious Creech from the saloon, the space created by the disturbance remained, and Levi found himself in direct view of the unruffled seated gambler.

"Well, gentlemen, it appears that due to an unforeseen incident we have an opportunity for someone to enhance their fortunes," Holliday exclaimed as he picked up and began to shuffle the pack.

"Do we have any takers, gentlemen?" Without moving his head, Holliday's eyes scanned across the apprehensive faces of the silent and discouraged. No one volunteered, and Holliday's gaze landed upon the Englishman.

"What about you, sir? Are you a gambler? You look capable of more than just occupying the chair vacated by the unfortunate Creech."

Levi knew he should ignore the younger man's taunting invite. He had only entered the bar to quell his inquisitiveness. He'd lost money, almost his own life, and his good friend had expelled his last breath at this exact bar.

He wasn't superstitious, but Van De Lyden's had never been a lucky drinking and gambling den for him in the past. However, he was now wiser and his fortunes had improved since he was last in Black Hawk, and so he chose to change the ill feelings and memories of misfortune, and he stepped forward to meet the challenge.

"I know my way around a deck of cards."

Levi stepped over the pool of Creech's blood and picked up a stool to replace the table stool.

"I fear I may have spooked the locals, but I can see from your reverence that you are not from the same spawn." Holliday held out a welcoming hand. "John Henry Holliday."

"Levi Clayton," Levi replied, accepting the handshake. Holliday noted the unfamiliar accent.

"I have a great curiosity, sir, to know whom I'm sharing a table with." He was assessing the stranger.

"My friends call me Lev." Levi did not oblige by enlightening Holliday or quench his inquisitiveness.

"Well, Lev, you do not have the grime of Black Hawk beguiling your features, and your tones are obviously not native, so from where do you hail, and may I enquire about what your business is here in this dullest of towns?"

"Come on, Doc. Time is a-wasting," urged the grey-whiskered man to Levi's left.

"Yeah, Doc. Get to dealing or I'm out of here," backed up the man to Levi's right.

"Doc?" Levi enquired. The people had changed, and some of the buildings had changed, but the scene and arguments remained the same even now fourteen years on.

"Yeah!" The grey-whiskered man cut in. "Trying to fool everybody by calling himself John Henry. But we all know him as Doc Holliday."

The name did not interest Levi. His attention had been seized by the coincidence that his friend, who died in almost the exact same spot, was also called 'Doc'.

"I'm not a doctor nor a dentist. I no longer have the genius for the trade."

Holliday wetted and flattened his moustache with his fingers, and then he spread the cards out into an arch in front of him with one hand. "This is my sport now."

He then swiftly collected them up again with the other hand and said, "Lev, this here is Ben Whitley and Heck Hensall."

Holliday introduced the two other gamblers as he split the deck and used both of his thumbs to fan the cards back into one stack. He then flipped them over, shuffled, cut, shuffled again, and placed the neat stack in front of Ben, and gave a brief nod. Ben split the stack by placing the top half of the cards to the right.

Heck picked up the left stack, placed it on top of the remaining deck, and dealt.

"Poker or Faro, Lev?" Holliday asked as he tried to subdue an irritating cough.

"I am adept at poker," Levi nodded.

This was an enjoyable challenge for Levi, but he had become accustomed to conquering the unknown, and a mere game of cards against two opponents who were already at a disadvantage by being glassy-eyed and laconic in speech would be a pushover.

He realised he must concentrate on bleeding the whisky-fuelled foundry men and avoid any direct confrontations with the perceived expert gambler seated directly opposite.

Doc Holliday stacked the old grimy cards, shuffled, cut, shuffled, paused to unfold a paisley handkerchief, and eventually dealt.

He then coughed brutally into the paisley cloth as each of the men gathered up their cards and, with frowning concentration, examined their hands with careful deliberation.

Heck Hensall, whose stubbled cheeks were pouching with a generous chew of tobacco, folded immediately. Ben opened with a ten-dollar bill whilst the others stayed in and exchanged one card each for one from the stack. Ben kept the ante at ten but folded when Levi and Holliday stayed in the game.

Holliday fanned his cards, released a smile, and then raised by ten. Heck, with his cigar clamped in the corner of his mouth, pushed another bill into the centre of the table. Holliday by now was not holding his cards; they were spread out on the table before him, and raising his glass to his lips, he tossed another note into the pot.

Heck stroked one side of his grey beard. A silver ring glistened, and he equalled the challenge. Holliday toyed with his money as he acted out a few moments of indecision, then lifted up another note and slid it across the table.

Two hours soon passed as the gamblers flipped cards, exchanged notes and coins, and cussed between them. Levi, Heck, and Ben drained three bottles of whisky, whilst Holliday had irritated all around with his repeated coughing.

Levi could no longer avoid a direct clash with Holliday, as between them, with deliberate and judicious wagers, they had bled Ben and Heck dry of all their hard-earned wealth.

Broken in spirit, the pair watched as Levi boldly raised the forty-dollar stakes to more than two hundred, and only Holliday opposed him in this final hand of high jeopardy.

Levi emptied the final droplets of whisky from the bottle into his shot glass.

"Looks like I'm all out, Holliday," Levi said, tossing in his final note and draining the glass.

"A shame that liquor robs a man of all reason. The toxicity infects his thoughts and pilfers his faculties," Holliday quipped, holding his gaze to his cards.

"Not this broth. It's not strong enough to even blister a man's throat," Levi admitted; his failings at the table were due to bad luck and poor judgement.

"Are you in, Lev?" Holliday teased with a confident smile.

"As I said, Holliday. I'm all out." Levi placed down his cards and stood up to pat his pockets to emphasise his position.

"What a shame, boys." Holliday's grin extended as he scanned across the loot and the disappointed faces of Ben and Heck.

"Hold on a darn minute, Holliday!" Heck held out his right arm as a barrier between Holliday and the cash, as his eyes had locked onto the LeMat which was tucked into Levi's belt. "What you got there, Lev?" he asked.

"Just some old shooter I picked up in Northfield." Levi was puzzled by Heck's interest and enthusiasm.

"That will cover the wager if Holliday agrees," Heck spurred. He was eager to see the infamous Doc Holliday finally lose.

"What?" Levi slid out the weapon and glared at the dull iron.

"Ah, come on, boys." Holliday gave only a brief glance at the weapon and leaned forward to scoop in the collection of coins and notes. "You've got to be jestin' with me. That tin pot ain't worth but a scratch."

"No, wait on there, Holliday," Heck insisted. "I've seen one of these before." He arched nearer to Levi to improve his view of the LeMat. "I was in Dodge back in '72, and a fella I knew sold one of these to a gun merchant for a high and mighty buck or two."

"Ah, come on, fellas. I'm calling it in." Holliday leaned forward again and circled his arms around the winnings. "But it's a shame, Lev, I was enjoying the contest."

Levi stood bemused, with his head lowered and his eyes engaged on the LeMat. His ears were filled with the sound of gunfire, and his thoughts were occupied with the dying faces of the outlaws and the young blonde-haired man lying in Northfield's dirt. He no longer heard the exchange of words between Heck or Holliday.

"Smiggers, get over here!" Heck called for the attention of a fellow drinker who was leaning on the bar. "Get over here and take a look at this."

He waved his arm to beckon the man to leave his station. Holliday shook his head slightly, sighed, and sat back in the chair with uninterested solace, but a sudden cough prevented him from collecting his winnings, and the delay gave Heck the time he needed to satisfy his curiosity.

Smiggers appeared through the bodies and stood at the side of the table. His face displayed a begrudging frown, confirming his displeasure at being drawn away from the comfort of the barstool.

"What in the hell do you want, Heck?" he grunted.

Heck did not reply. He merely gave a single nod in the direction of Levi's hand.

"Holy moly," Smiggers' jaw dropped. "Mind if I take a look at that, fella?" Levi did not notice the appearance of the heavy man standing to his side, and he failed to respond.

Smiggers looked into the stranger's blank eyes and slowly lifted the weapon, unchallenged, from Levi's hand.

"A God darn LeMat!" Suddenly the brooding pout disappeared and the man's round face flushed and beamed with enthusiasm. "Never thought I'd see one of these beauties again." He angled it in his hand high towards the lamp. "Just needs polishing up all pretty."

"What's it worth?" asked Heck.

Smiggers did not reply to Heck. His eyes absorbed the piece as his fingers feathered and caressed the cold iron.

"Erm, quite a find these days," he said, looking down. "Issued to only the elite in the rebel army—generals and officers and such like." He educated them in almost a trance-like state.

"Yeah, but what's it worth?" Heck hurriedly prompted again.

"Is it for sale, fella?" Smiggers finally spurted.

"Not yet, but it may well be in a minute or two." Holliday was now interested and his face raised from his handkerchief.

"Are you selling, fella?" Smiggers addressed Levi directly.

"Erm…" Levi hesitated and could not reply as Heck impatiently bellowed again, this time stepping up close to Smiggers.

"What's its God-darn worth?"

"Hard to rightly tell."

"Cover the ante?" Holliday pressed, nodding at the wealth.

"My guess is that you could treble what's on the table and not get nowhere near its true value."

Suddenly, the room quietened and everyone became interested.

"And may I ask what gives you the credentials to be an expert?" quipped Holliday, now his curiosity was aroused.

"Excuse me." Smiggers looked up from the LeMat and gave an expression revealing he did not like the connotation in the direction of the seated gambler.

"Pay no notion to him, Smiggers." Heck positioned himself in front of Smiggers and added to Holliday's interest. "He owns the gun and ammunition store on Miners Street."

"Well then, sir… I'm obliged for your expertise and service on this unexpectedly pleasant evening," Holliday fanned his hand at Smiggers and confidently dismissed the gunsmith's involvement.

Shrugging his shoulders, Smiggers muttered his annoyance and turned to walk back to the bar.

"Well then, are you in, Mister Lev… or do you fold?"

No one saw Sheriff Kelton return to the saloon, and no one paid him any attention as he watched the gamblers from a discreet unlit corner.

187

He did not like the brash young gambler who seemed to prey on the weak, gullible foundry workers and fleece them of their hard-earned coins with ease, and the seated stranger with the distinct accent irked him.

He narrowed his eyes to improve his vision across the room and drew in a large breath to clear his mind of any prejudiced perceptions that might hinder his powers of recall. Slowly, very slowly, his thoughts cast back to a cold winter many years previous.

Standing before him and pleading for freedom from behind the solid bars of the town cell was a young man named Levi Clayton.

The Sheriff could now recall with vivid detail the Englishman he had arrested for the murder of a man whose face he could not recall. He was intrigued by the man's return and perplexed why this murderer was risking his life by returning to Black Hawk.

He had learned earlier in the day that the stranger had visited the cemetery to fund the installation of a headstone for a long-time dead doctor called Fergus McCurdy, and he wondered why. What relationship did this stranger have with the long-since murdered man, he mused.

The Sheriff watched the events unfurl in the gambler's den. There was nothing unusual about the proceedings or the activities of the night.

Every night played out the same. Men got drunk, gambled away their money, and then the laughter turned to rapid loose tongues, which led to fist fights, gunfire, and bloodshed.

This was a very ordinary night, with the exception that an accused murderer had returned to the town after almost fifteen years of freedom. The Sheriff could not understand the man's motive for the return; he could have organised the instalment of a memorial from afar. He recalled the last time he saw the Englishman's face as he walked out from the cells of Black Hawk, a free man upon the insistence of a Union captain who was in the area conscripting troops to squash a brigade of rebels who had assembled in the pines on the edge of the mountains.

Many years later, Kelton learned the Union captain was a fraud, and he had been duped into releasing the Englishman with another man who was an associate of the fake captain. Now the unexpected events of the past day had given Sheriff Kelton the opportunity to finally administer justice to the Englishman. He unholstered his Remington and began to make his way through the crowded revellers.

"Where the hell is he, Holliday?" Kelton's eyes became alert at the empty chair at the table. His gaze flashed a menacing glare across the faces of Ben and Heck until it settled on Holliday.

189

"May I be of some assistance to you, Sheriff?" Holliday's face beamed a huge smile as he forced his eyes up from his newly acquired LeMat to look at the intimidating Sheriff.

"Where is he?" His face stoned as he roared loudly.

"And to whom are you referring, Sheriff?" Holliday's reply was delivered with a goading tease.

The Sheriff's rage was clear and Ben and Heck remained silent. They had no idea what had incensed the Sheriff and they dared not ask.

"You God-darn well know who—the Englishman. Where the hell is he?" Kelton banged his fist hard on the table, causing the stacks of coins to topple and Ben and Heck to step back in alarm, whilst Holliday began coughing violently and repetitively into his handkerchief, delaying his reply to the annoyance of the Sheriff.

"Well sir, if you are referring to my friend Lev," he paused to cough again, "he figured he had run right out of luck tonight and it was time for him to depart before the night turned too damn sour for his taste."

"Where has he gone?" Kelton spat with urgency. "Did he tell you where he was going?"

“That, sir, he did not confer,” Holliday replied with an almost baiting grin, and the Sheriff reacted instantly by flipping the table and shouting,

“Get the hell out of my town, fang doctor!”

He shouldered past the crowd and lunged into the night after the escaped convict. The saloon's glow vanished behind him as the door slammed shut, cutting him off from the noise and revelry in an instant and leaving him alone in the darkness and silence of the deserted street.

Chapter 8

November 7th 1887

John 'Doc' Henry Holliday stretched himself on the mattress. Pain spasmed through his entire body. He was no longer the immaculately presented and scrupulously neat gambler of years past.

The days of being a ruthless high roller and a cynical, deadly killer lay well behind him, and he knew there could be no return to the wild nights for the once popular master of both the deck and the gun. He now lay a weak specimen of human insignificance. His body was wreaked by illness and years of being a profligate drunk. He was emaciated, his hollow face drained of all colour, and his once fierce eyes now sunk and circled by black recesses.

The room was bare of all furnishings, long sold off to pay for his treatment: the lavish mahogany bureau, Navajo rugs, ornate framed oil paintings, and the dressing table with the large French mirror. He could not see his skeletal face and jaundiced skin, which had been ravaged by consumption.

The venom from the decay infected and warped his thoughts, and reality often merged into hallucinations with bouts of violent coughing fits which exhausted him.

Constant cold sweats and uncontrollable diarrhoea made him uncomfortably sore and damp, and his pillow and sheets were stained with the disease.

Slowly he raised his head and craned his neck to scan the dimly lit room. As normal, there were no visitors or carers in attendance. He was no longer the in-demand famed gambler; he was a forgotten man. He frowned to help clear his vision, but he could see nothing to interest him until his eyes locked onto his gun belt, which was draped across the bed chair next to him.

At first, his stiffened muscles refused to obey him as he painfully reached out to grab the handle of the LeMat, but he continued to reach out with gritted determination until phlegm spilled out of the side of his mouth and splattered onto the bare floor below.

The effort distressed him and forced him to release a piteous groan. He paused for a moment, drew in a large breath, and then stretched out again until his bony fingers were locked around the walnut handle.

Withdrawing the holstered pistol and guiding it back towards him, he let out another yell of anguish, as the sustained effort had been too great for him, and his head and limbs sagged, leaving his overworked lungs panting for breath.

Finally, he sagged into a shapeless heap on the bed, and with a pained expression on his white face, he settled into silence as his fingers glided along the etchings on the LeMat.

A small indication of a smile creased his sullen cheeks as he found comfort in holding the treasured weapon. He could not recall how long he had owned the pistol nor how he came to own it, but he could recall feeling the force of its blast in the palm of his hand.

He tried to call out for help, but the words caught in his throat, and only drool and phlegm, followed by a mouthful of vomit, were spat out instead of the plea that he intended.

His insides felt as though they had been sliced with a blade, and they burned like something from hell. The vile stench of his detriment pierced his nostrils, and the shock of realising his invincibility had finally departed his spirit left him almost paralysed in his incapacitated body. With great effort, he forced his mind back to a memory long ago.

"Oh, my lovelies, aren't I going to have some fun time pleasuring you two delights tonight." Holliday grinned as he buried his face into the exposed breasts of Maribella.

"Oh yeah, Mister Holliday. We know how to work the tenderloin and we are gonna ride you like we're at the rodeo," confirmed Annie Lou into Holliday's ear as she wrapped her silk stocking-covered legs around his waist.

Stimulated by alcohol and energised from a successful night at the Faro table, the red-eyed gambler was wedged on his hotel bed between Dodge City's two most renowned and expensive whores.

Holliday swigged another mouthful of cheap whisky and then lowered the bottle carefully next to his feet as the kneeling Maribella began to smother him with kisses, while Annie Lou trapped his willing body between her legs from the rear. Wrapping her arms around to his front, she began to unfasten his damp and sweaty shirt.

"Dear Lord, indulge me for tonight, I'm going to heaven," he whispered, looking up towards the yellow glowing chandelier.

Maribella paused for breath, and as she relaxed, Holliday cupped and groped her oversized breasts with both of his hands. She feigned a pleasurable moan and released the buckle on his belt, then she pulled on the leather until it enabled her to toss the strapping over her shoulder. The LeMat thudded hard against the bare wood bedstead, and it spilled out from its holster and slid across the floorboards.

"Whoa there, sweetheart," Holliday slurred. "Take it easy with the valuables."

"Don't you be worrying yourself about that, Doc. I know how to handle a man's weapon," she teased, her red lips curving upwards as she grabbed hard at his groin.

"At a hundred bucks a piece, I'm sure you God-darn well do."

Holliday didn't care that Annie Lou and Maribella's sexual ardour and sultry glances were fake.

He knew of their profession and reputation, but with ample winnings still bulging in his pockets, he intended to end this night with a passionate encounter which would fulfil his yearning desires and render him breathless by sexual exertion instead of the nightly bouts of coughing which had crept upon him over the past few months.

Ignoring Holliday's gibe, Maribella arched slightly backwards, exposing her huge mounds of flesh. She shook her shoulders to wiggle her breasts to Holliday's delight.

"Oh, my Lord," he hissed to himself, thrusting his face forward to slip perfectly into the separating gorge of cleavage.

"Can I play in this party?" Annie Lou enticed, pulling Holliday back towards her into her lap.

Without the need for instruction or further words, Maribella knew what her partner was alluding to, and urging the willing gambler to arch to one side, she leaned forward and met the approaching lips, allowing the women to lock their mouths together.

"The devil has gotten into us all tonight," Holliday muttered deliriously.

Without breaking from the embrace, Maribella hooked her arm around Annie Lou's neck and pulled the lace to release her tight corset and expose her perfectly formed bosom. Holliday slid lower to adjust his position so that he could improve his view as Maribella guided her head closer to Annie Lou's flesh and dragged her tongue across from one nipple to the other.

He gawked as Maribella flicked and kissed each nipple until they were erect and ready to be engulfed by her warm mouth. Both Holliday and Annie Lou released a gasp of pleasure as her nipple disappeared into Maribella's red lips.

Spasms of excitement coursed through Holliday's loins as he watched the women's embrace build to a crescendo of passion. He momentarily broke away from the performance to grab the half-empty bottle of whisky, and, managing to slant his eyes back on the women, he deliriously gulped down the burning liquid.

Releasing the bottle, his increased cravings urged him to join the frantic embrace, and with expert, predetermined timing, Maribella twisted her face and grabbed the back of his neck to guide their mouths together. The three semi-naked bodies writhed together as the increasing passion dominated their actions, until a shudder of bewilderment ran down Holliday's spine which instantly banished the fervour.

His body firmed rigid as he felt the cold steel of his LeMat press hard into the back of his neck. Immediately, all the semi-naked writhing stopped as the six eyes opened wide and glared at the pistol-wielding women. Holliday slowly withdrew his head from the breast of Annie Lou and turned his head to the side.

"Ah, my darling Kate." He knew the fun was prematurely over. "Come to join the frivolity?"

'Big Nose' Kate Elder, Doc Holliday's lover, friend, partner, and carer for the last five years did not reply. Her face stunned a look of injustice and hatred at the pair of giggling whores.

"Well, climbing in or not?" Holliday's rationale was non-existent due to his mind being flooded with a consumption of passion, his blood poisoned with excessive alcohol. He could not resist the urge to tease his long-suffering companion.

"You lousy, no good son of a worthless bitch."

Without breaking away from the glare, Kate reached down, grabbed, and raised the whisky bottle.

Quickly glancing through the green glass at the remnants, she added. "You weak bastard. You just can't leave it alone, can you?" She then hurled the bottle in the direction of the wall behind the bed and screamed. "Get the hell out of here, you low-down stinking tramps."

Belatedly ducking and covered in whisky spray and broken glass, Holliday stammered, "Now just hold on a minute, Kate." He held up both his hands in a defensive manner. "Don't be so hasty. We're just having a bit of fun. It don't mean nothing serious." He grinned.

"I hate you." She spat.

"Ah, come on, you ought to try it sometime."

Kate responded by swinging the barrel of the LeMat across the side of Holliday's face so hard that it knocked him clear off the bed and left a spray of blood across the two whores' flesh.

Shrieks and screams of shock were released in unison from the prostitutes who were now embraced in each other's arms, rigid with fear.

"What!" Kate raged, tossing the discarded bodices in their direction. "What are you all waiting for? Get out! Get out of here now!"

Although numbed by the sudden and violent intervention, both the whores were toughened by the ways of the rough life they had chosen and, now regaining their composure, they remained virtually unmoved.

"Compensation," Maribella said, folding her arms under her drooping breasts in defiance.

"What?" Kate scowled, her forehead furrowing with lines of bemusement.

"Yes…. compensation," said Maribella, "for loss of earnings."

"We've already worked darn hard on this loser," Annie Lou added as she wrapped the corset around her. "And if you hadn't come in here all carrying on and hollering like a wild pole cat, we would have earned enough greenbacks to see the month out."

Holliday had begun to unsteadily rise onto his knees. He rubbed away the line of fresh blood where a lump was forming and shook his head to try and clear his blurred vision.

"You God-darn lousy miserable bitches," Kate began as she levelled the pistol in their direction. "You get the hell out of here fast or I guarantee you both, the next time you two will be on your backs is when you're taking a ride in old Prescott's hearse." She steadied her aim. "Now get. Get out now!"

Maribella and Annie Lou knew Kate to be a straight talker with a reputation for regular outbursts of violence and, when her normally placid temper had been stirred, they knew it was wise not to test her fortitude any further.

"Only jealous 'cause you're not earning tonight," quipped Maribella as she deliberately bumped into Kate's shoulder on her way to the open door, which was now blocked with curious and enthusiastic onlookers.

Eyes gaping wide, the throng made up mainly of men moved to form a semicircle to allow the two disrobed whores to pass through.

"Don't look at what you can't afford to buy boys," Maribella said as she scowled one last look behind her and into the bedroom as she disappeared into the congested corridor.

Kate directed far fewer words at the audience as she kicked the door closed. "Feck off!"

"Take no care of them, honey," Holliday said, as he swayed on the edge of the bed, waving a beckoning hand. "Come on Kate, there's no need to be like this," he added when her sternness failed to soften.

"I was just having a little harmless fun time." He had to rest his arm on the footboard to steady himself and prevent his legs from giving way.

201

"Why, you lousy ungrateful bastard!" She raised the LeMat in his direction and contemplated boring a hole in his forehead. "Shut your God-darn shit-talking mouth. I don't know why I've put up with you all these wasted years."

She was humiliated and an evil resilience from within urged her not to kill him, but to let him live to suffer years of agony whilst his body wasted slowly away with consumption.

"Ah come on Kate. You know I would have been with you tonight, but I didn't know where you were at." Now he dropped his buttocks back on the bed.

"You lying poisonous snake." Her patience and resolve were being tested, and she could not prevent her fingers from tensing on the trigger. "You had no intentions of comforting me since we came to this God-darn hellhole of a place."

"Now you know that's not true, honey," Holliday lied.

"Shut your mouth and hold your tongue, you worthless shit. Those two leeches would have taken you for every cent you own."

"Huh, well I was just about to make sure they God-darn earned it," Holliday tried to subdue his drunken giggle. "You know my ways in the sack." He knew he should not taunt Kate nor treat her this way, but his words and actions were still induced by intoxication and his lusty desires were still unabated.

“Bastard!”

“Come on Kate. Climb in.” He was not oblivious to Kate’s fury, but he could not control his obsessive selfish ardour. He nodded towards the dishevelled bed.

“My pecker’s already as hard as solid oak,” he proudly grinned and grabbed his crotch area.

“You lowlife waster. Have you no shame or remorse?” She had been with the gambler long enough to know he felt no indignity, and he was oblivious to the lurid side of his reputation. “Everything I have done for you and you do not show one notion of regret.”

Her mind was occupied with the long and endless nights where she cared for his rehabilitation and recumbence from the now regular exhaustive fits of coughing brought on by the increasing sapping bouts of consumption.

“When I think about all the years of my lie I have wasted by your sick, lonely side…”

She took a step towards him, still slanting the pistol in his direction, “All for nothing, no gratitude, no serenity or love.” She again took another step forward. “Well, to hell with you John Henry Fecking Holliday. I’m done with emptying your piss bowl, wiping away your drool and mopping your fecking brow.”

"How dare you!" Holliday tried, but failed to rise from the bed.

He was offended by her verbal onslaught. He considered himself in higher esteem and superior to an unattached woman of her status, and their relationship was that of a master-and-servant co-existence in which she should be grateful and honoured to serve the renowned and legendary 'Doc Holliday'.

"I pay you well for your services, do I not?"f

Holliday's comment thrust deep pain throughout Kate's core. She now knew he considered her stature the same as many other wives and partners in these unforgiving towns, where many women had to rely on providing other benefits to men folk, including selling sex, to generate enough income for basic survival.

The thought wrenched her stomach, and she glared in disdain at the vile man who she mistakenly thought respected her and only offered her support in the same way a married man would give his wife money.

Sudden darkness fell upon Holliday.

He did not see Kate swing the barrel of the LeMat in his direction, nor did he hear his skull crack against the steel. He was unconscious and oblivious to the last words of Kate Elder. "Matthew 5:38... eye for an eye and tooth for a tooth. Now go to hell!"

A loud involuntary rumble issued from his stomach brought Holliday once more back into reality. Riveting pain still dictated his every breath and, so carefully and very slowly, he tried to gather spittle in his parched mouth to ease the burning dryness that seemed to rise from the pit of the stomach to the top of his throat. He cared little for survival and he had lost all gusto for adventures, which he knew there was to be no return. Sweats and chronic pain riddled his slumber, and he was now embittered by the dreams which tormented him of his former life of self-indulgence.

He fought against the pain to crack open an eyelid to the brightness of the afternoon sun whose rays warmed his bed, but spiralling spasms of excruciation flashed up from his back to his head and temples, resulting in him holding tight his eyelids in an effort to gain a moment of relief. The pain spread to his chest and an all-consuming misery that ravaged throughout his every nerve and fibre, and within seconds his vision blurred and darkness descended again as the first solaces of oblivion began to relieve the impelling affliction.

No one was paying any attention to the late afternoon sun as its glow began to gradually subside in the clear blue sky over Tombstone.

Crowds were gathering on the boardwalks and at the corners of the streets as unrest had begun to quickly spread.

Rumours and speculation that a confrontation between the Earp brothers and the Clanton and McLaury gang were now widespread amongst the residents, gamblers and tradesmen of Tombstone. Most of them were eager to see an end to the hell raisers who had grown wild on the open range and regularly infested the town to let loose their boredom with drunken anarchy and debauchery.

Tongues were eagerly conveying welcomed messages that the Earp's had tolerated enough of this wild behaviour and that a confrontation with the gang of outlaws was imminent. A bloody climax was now inevitable and an uneasy hush had settled around Fremont Street as the fear of gunplay and death increased as noon had turned slowly into late afternoon.

Doc Holliday was seated in his usual chair in the Alhambra Saloon when the whisperers reached his ears. Due to the usual late night of gambling, he had slept away the morning and most of the afternoon and he had missed much of the excited gossip. He knew the relationship between the Earp's and the Clanton's had soured over the past few months and throughout the previous evening, Ike Clanton had been in Tombstone shouting out insults about Wyatt Earp to everyone who frequented the drinking holes along Allen Street, Fourth, and Toughnut.

At some point after midnight, Holliday himself took to defending his friend Wyatt's reputation directly with Ike and, in the heat of the argument, Holliday threatened Ike and challenged him to a duel.

Holliday knew Ike would not meet the challenge alone. He had an avarice for causing trouble, but he did not have the lethal natural talent to back up his foolhardiness.

Holliday smiled as he recalled the gutless gape on Ike's face as he discreditably scampered out of the Crystal Palace Saloon to disappear into the darkness.

Holliday finished off his all-day breakfast and draped his long grey coat over his favourite light grey suit.

The late October chill needled at his back and aggravated his lungs, often rendering him with ceaseless bouts of painful hacking. Reaching the door, he would decide whether it was necessary to fully fasten up or just risk the covering of the cloak as he strutted, his silver-headed cane tapping loudly with every step on the timber floor towards his next liquor house.

Stepping out on the planks, he was met by three of the Earp brothers: Virgil, Wyatt, and Morgan. Dressed with their black stetsons pulled low to protect their vision from the low sun, the lawmen wore matching black greatcoats and string ties which hung loosely down over their white shirts.

Holliday noted the solemnity which was etched on their stern countenances, and he instantly knew the seriousness of their concern.

"Is this it, Virgil?" he asked, referring to noticeable tension and increasing conjecture.

"There is nothing to interest a drunk," rebuked Morgan. "Now go back inside and care for your own business."

Holliday defiantly stood firm, preventing the Earp's from continuing their journey down the decking.

"I'm not deaf to the threats, Morgan," he replied.

"It's time, Doc," Virgil affirmed, narrowing his eyes as he spoke. "The climate has boiled over." Virgil slanted his face left then right to glance quickly at both Wyatt and Morgan. "We need more guns, boys," he warned.

Holliday smiled and slightly bowed his head in the direction of Wyatt and Morgan.

Virgil Earp was the marshal of Tombstone and his large frame and tactile demeanour had warmed him to law-demanding folks of Tombstone. To cleanse Tombstone of violence, Virgil had sworn in his younger brothers as deputy sheriff and deputy marshal.

Wyatt was renowned for his deft and decisive approach to taming dangerous and reckless behaviour, and Morgan's pursuit of tracking fleeing outlaws was applauded throughout Arizona.

"You drunk, Doc?" Virgil asked, glaring directly into his red-veined yellow eyes.

"I'm standing, aren't I?" he replied, opening out his hands and slightly bending his legs to half-curtsy.

Virgil did not reply; instead, he struck a match to his pipe which was clamped between his teeth.

"This is not your fight, Doc," Wyatt stated.

"We are short of officials here, Wyatt," Virgil emphasised again, puffing out a cloud of smoke.

Aware that the presence of the notorious deadly dentist would further decrease the resolution and defiance of the Clanton and McLaury brothers, Wyatt studied Holliday's poise, and he was confident he was not yet ruined by drink, but it was Morgan who cut in. "This may not be pleasant, Doc."

"I have a disdain for cowardly loudmouths and besides, I like a dead man after my breakfast," Holliday's eyes and mouth widened.

"There's no call for you in this mix, Doc." Wyatt knew he was wasting his words. His friend was absolutely fearless, possibly mentally unbalanced, but he was loyal to the Earp's, and Wyatt knew Holliday would press his opinions and not waver from his decisions. Still, he backed Morgan's objection.

Holliday fixed Wyatt with a stare, his brow furrowing and his eyes widening as he raised his voice. "That's a hell of a thing for you to say to me, Wyatt." He tapped the walnut grip of his holstered LeMat, the gesture betraying a resolve that was rapidly hardening.

He had been at Wyatt's side on many occasions when skilful and lethal gunplay had been required, and he felt a sense of honour that he was not prepared to betray. Neither was he going to surrender or yield from his principles.

"I will not neglect my duties. Now swear me in, Virgil, and let me at that bothersome blabbermouth Ike Clanton."

Virgil conveyed his approval with a slight nod and he grasped the cane from Holliday's hand. "Here, keep this out of sight." In exchange, he handed Holliday his sawn-off shotgun.

"God darn it," Wyatt muttered, and Holliday returned a smile.

Quietly, the four men stepped out onto the street and began to walk shoulder to shoulder towards Fremont Street in search of the Clanton's and McLaury's.

No one spoke as they paced the dirt of Fourth Street, passing the post office and the Capital Saloon. Standing erect with stride matching stride, eyes locked unnervingly ahead, and their hands clasped around their concealed pistols, they did not let the gathering townsfolk distract them from their focus.

At the corner of Fremont Street, Holliday and the Earp's caught sight of their foe.

Idling at the side of Harwood's house were Ike Clanton, Billy Clanton, Billy Claiborne, Frank McLaury, and Tom McLaury.

The Earp's glare was broken as Sheriff John Behan stepped out in front of them waving his hands.

"Don't you fellas leave here. I'll take care of this," he shouted.

Although Behan was Virgil Earp's commanding officer, the Earp's considered him weak, pretentious, and mistrustful.

"The hell you will not," shouted Wyatt, and ignoring Behan's order, the four men continued with their composed stride as Behan turned heel and sped in the direction of the Clanton's waving his arms above his head.

The lawmen continued their advance; no signs of fear or anxiety were displayed. Stetsons had to be pulled even lower to protect their concentrated vision from interfering glare as the low sun reflected flashes of blinding brilliance from the passing windows.

Whispered apprehensive comments mixed with cautionary calls of encouragement could be heard from gathering bystanders on the boardwalks who were following on behind to see what would occur next, many of them pretending to be brave but distancing themselves far enough back to betray their bravado.

Holliday tipped his hat and smiled at some of the spectators, but he did not see who the acknowledgement was directed at; his eyes only saw the desperados ahead.

In the distance, someone hollered out, "Here they come!"

A breeze caught Holliday's coat, and it flapped open revealing the shotgun to the accompanying sighs of shock from witnesses to his side.

"Let them have it, Doc!" was called out from an unknown insensitive face and without diverting his gaze, Holliday nodded and gritted his reply.

"Well, alright then."

Wyatt watched Behan gesturing with Ike Clanton. He was still waving his arms in a foreboding manner as if he did not want Ike to move, but as he turned to face the nearing lawmen Wyatt read his lips.

"Stay put whilst I see to these clowns."

Wyatt bit hard on his clenched teeth and flexed his fingers around the handle of his pistol as Behan ran to meet them under the shading of Bauer's meat market awning.

"Stop right here, fellas," he spat out, trying to regain his breath with a torrent of sweat dripping from his brow.

"Don't be afraid, Johnny," Virgil sneered in a calm, low tone, "we don't want trouble. I'm just going to disarm them."

Virgil stiff-armed Behan to his side and continued walking.

"I've disarmed them!" he shouted to Virgil's back. "There's no need for you to go down there."

Now Wyatt stood directly in front of Behan. "We're going to set things right, Johnny." He too pushed Behan to the side and continued walking.

"Earp, for God's sake. I'm telling you, don't go down there."

The call did not alter the gait of the gunmen.

"Get back here, Virgil. I'm the sheriff of this county." Still, Behan persisted, but the four shooters all ignored his weak attempt to stop the confrontation and, wanting to escape prying eyes who had witnessed the undermining embarrassment, he quickly slipped into the shadows of the nearest back alley.

Virgil paused to tap out his pipe on a porch support and said, "OK boys, nice and calm. I'll do the talking." He then slipped the pipe into his inner coat pocket.

Wyatt stretched out his fingers on his right hand, and then tightened his fist into a ball; he repeated this quickly several times to ensure his grip and aim would be true.

Silence had descended upon Fremont and all that could be heard was the leather of the lawmen's boots compacting the dirt as they marched in unison towards their foe.

The Clanton's and McLaury's attentions were now fixed on the four approaching men.

Without speaking, Billy Claiborne turned and ran in the direction of the O.K. Corral, but the remaining four gunmen cast fearless looks to each other, confirming their intentions of meeting the Earp's challenge.

They stepped forward and filled their lungs to the maximum with Tombstone air to intimidatingly expand their frames as they held an unyielding stance.

Now less than six feet away from their foe, Virgil stepped into the front of the menaces and, holding Holliday's cane above his head with his right hand, he shouted:

"Throw up your hands. We're here to disarm you."

There was no time for evasive tactics and no place to hide. It was time to either yield or resolve by the ritual obligatory gunfire and inevitable bloodshed.

A click from Billy's and Frank's direction broke the fleeting silence as they cocked their holstered pistols.

"Hold on, boys. I don't want this!" Virgil's alarmed eyes widened, and he waved the cane above his head to distract everyone and prevent the withdrawal of weapons. "All I want is your guns."

No one moved, but eyes flashed across trembling fingers and stern faces as the tension simmered, all knowing that if anyone drew weapons, there would be no stopping the bloodletting and death.

"Son of a bitch!" Wyatt breathed as he watched Billy's hand tighten around his pistol.

The indecision was broken, and gunfire immediately erupted.

Billy shot at Wyatt, but Wyatt reacted by slanting his body in Frank's direction. He knew Billy had a youthful foolishness, and this made him dangerous, but he also knew Frank was the best shot in the gang, so he had already decided he would shoot Frank first.

Billy's lead sped through the air and missed Wyatt as he arched quickly to draw and fire his Smith & Wesson.

215

Frank grabbed his coat lapels and pulled open his coat to reach for his weapon, but releasing a cry of anguish, his body folded as Wyatt's aim was precise and his bullet tore deep into Frank's stomach before he had time to level his aim. Staggering backwards with blood spurting high, Frank dropped his pistol and fell face down.

Virgil stood exposed with Doc's cane in his gun hand as shots erupted from all directions.

Dust clouded up from the ground and wood splinters sprayed from the impact of mis-aimed bullets as the slaughter commenced.

Ike began to panic, and he ran at Wyatt.

Not long ago he had swanked courage, but now he trembled with fright. He tried to grab Wyatt's pistol but, being accustomed to fist fights and with superior strength and size, Wyatt easily pushed him aside and down to the ground.

"The fighting has commenced," Wyatt raged down at the coward.

"Don't shoot me," spittle spurted from Ike's mouth as he frantically pleaded for his life.

"Go to fighting or get away," Wyatt calmly commanded, forcing his boot into Ike's midriff.

Ike scrambled to his feet and, waving his arms in desperation, he began to flee in the same direction as Billy Claiborne.

Meanwhile, and simultaneously, in the mayhem, Morgan had opened up repeated fire at Billy's head, but his aim was low and Billy was blasted backwards as bullets thundered into his chest and slammed his body so hard into the wooden panels of Harwood's house that he shattered the window.

Billy's hand flapped loose and blood sprayed as another bullet fractured wide open his right wrist, and sliding to the floor with screams of agony, he released his gun to the soil.

Tom had ducked down low and sought protection behind his horse, but as he aimed at Wyatt, Holliday fired his shotgun into the air above the horse, causing it to bolt and expose him. Both men locked onto each other and began to aim.

Holliday coolly pulled back the hammer and levelled the sawn-off ten-gauge, then he released the ominous click to blast Tom in the side with buckshot as a retaliatory shot bellowed past his ear and disappeared safely into the sky.

With blood oozing out of his peppered shirt, Tom staggered in retreat onto Fremont Street, unable to clear his vision or regain his breath.

Smoke clouded low and dimmed the bright afternoon rays, which had only moments earlier warmed the cool October breeze around the corner of the O.K. Corral, Fremont Street, and Harwood's house.

Ears hummed as the sound of repeated gunfire reverberated and the narrowed eyes of the shootists smarted from the acrid bellowing gunpowder as the slaughter continued.

Frank raged in pain from his wound, but he managed to stagger to his feet and desperately lunged at a fleeing horse, grabbing hold of the rifle in the scabbard.

Holliday caught sight of Frank and he threw down his empty shotgun and reached for his LeMat as he watched the bloodied man begin to level the rifle and take aim.

"You're mine now, Holliday! I've got you now, you lousy no-good son of a bitch," he threatened as smoke bellowed from the rifle.

Holliday staggered as he felt a burning pain in his hip, but biting his teeth down hard, he continued to walk forward directly towards Frank.

At that moment he felt indestructibly reckless, and he mocked, "Blaze away, Frank," he yelled as he finally withdrew and raised the LeMat. "You'll be a daisy if you can take me."

Morgan had also seen Frank aiming at Holliday. He switched aim from Billy to fire the last of his bullets at the dangerous gunman and simultaneously Morgan's pistol and Holliday's LeMat burst lead into Frank, throwing him back and high. With a hole below his ear and another in his chest, Frank was dead before his limp body thundered down onto the ground.

In the midst of the gun battle Virgil had shifted the cane to his other hand and began to fumble around near his holster for his pistol whilst gasping for life. Billy had managed to pick up and level his pistol across his folded legs with his left hand.

From the imposed recumbent position, he squinted through his flooded eyes and shot at the indecisive Virgil. Calling out and twisting with pain, Virgil dropped his pistol. He initially fought hard to keep his balance, but he buckled and dropped to the floor as Billy's gunshot tore through his ankle.

Holliday caught a glimpse of the shooting, and holding out his LeMat firm, he angled his forward walk slowly in the direction of Billy.

"You shot my friend. Now I am going to kill you," he baited.

Wyatt, now satisfied Ike was no longer of concern, twisted back towards the shootout where he sighted Virgil stumbling onto his knees, then his attention was drawn towards the incensed Billy who ignored Holliday to aim at Morgan.

Instantaneously both Wyatt and Holliday unleashed their pistols at the same time, blasting several holes into Billy's chest, but with relentless determination, Billy ensured he fired his final shot with accuracy into Morgan's shoulder.

"I am hit!" Morgan yelled as he stumbled back from the impact of the missile.

Now striding to within touching distance of Billy, Holliday calmly watched the blood-drenched Billy swivel his pistol in his direction and pull again on the trigger, but this time only the click of the metal hammer could be heard as the exhausted chamber failed to fire.

"Give me some more cartridges to finish this fight," Billy wheezed, a mouthful of blood spilling as his dim red eyes rolled towards Holliday.

Ignoring the blood-soaked dying man, Holliday lifted the pistol from his loose hand and declared to his friend by his side,

"You know, Wyatt, I've yet to hear a man squeal when he is about to die."

"Then you have yet to kill a coward," Wyatt stated, bowing his head towards the dying young man.

A groaning death rattle was finally released and Billy's head sagged limply sideways, allowing his mouth to release yet more blood, and his slitty eyes to stare blankly into the red soil at his side.

The shooting was over, but the confusion was not. Holliday placed his palm across his hip and he felt a hot patch of blood where he had been wounded. Virgil tried to raise and balance himself on Holliday's cane and the uninjured Wyatt knelt at Morgan's side to assess the seriousness of the puncture.

Thick gun smoke drifted over the now almost silent bloodied battlefield.

Tom McLaury could be heard in the distance vomiting as he choked to death on blood. Billy was slouched against Harwood's house and Frank lay motionless face down in a pooling circle of claret.

The thirty seconds of slaughter would be imprinted on the backs of the survivors' eyelids for the remainder of their lives; whenever they dozed, relaxed, and slept, the mayhem would be there to relive over and over again.

Sheriff John Behan and Billy Claiborne began to approach through the clearing smoke.

"Nobody move! You're all coming with me," he ordered.

Struggling to contain his anger, Wyatt rose from Morgan's side and pushed Behan hard in the chest.

"We will not be arrested by you today, Sheriff," Wyatt warned, and he continued the pushing momentum.

Behan recognised Wyatt was far beyond any reconciliation, and he allowed himself to be forced backward and away from the scene. Claiborne remained silent and gawked at his dead friends.

Onlookers began to walk through the barbarous scene, stopping to gawk at the dead and scour for souvenirs. The proud Earp brothers and Holliday looked solemn in the presence of death and they watched numbly as spent cartridges, pieces of clothing, hats, and guns were looted.

An excited, fresh-faced boy said something to Holliday, but he failed to recognise the words because he was still deafened by the thunder of the gunfire. He did, however, cast a smile down at the kid and gave him a candy bar from his pocket.

Holliday had once again readily allowed his mind to become possessed by the alchemy caused by shock and pain. As one image would gradually lose its perfection and begin to disappear, another would arise from its fusion until once more his fevered mind was occupied with happy reminiscences.

He now understood why his mind had been occupied with past events of his life and that recollections of times past were all that he was surviving on.

He had acknowledged he was now in the final chapter of his life and, with pain beyond all control, he once more readily submitted to the state of unconscious remises to allow his mind to drift back to a time in Denver as he awaited the inevitable shroud of death to enclose its vices upon him.

Here, as in every dream, the weather seemed warmer, the sky bluer, the clouds more sparse and the food and drink more tasty and satisfying.

"The drinks are on me!"

The deep throated offer was greeted with a huge cheer, and the accompanying mass hat waving.

"I can lick any man in the whole world," the burly man boasted loudly as he spiritedly barged into the barroom of the Buckhorn Hotel and approached the counter surrounded by half a dozen of his associates.

Holliday was seated in his usual booth close to the bar. He had drunk too much, as was his custom. The strong spirits were now the only substance that dulled the pain, eased his repeating cough, and helped him get through the day.

He was desperately short of funds and so, for the first time in his life, he had betrayed his principles. In the past, he vowed he would never speak to correspondents and reporters, but now, in these desperate times where he could not earn a living due to the undesired effects of his illness, he was preparing to sell his life story to a news reporter who worked for the Rocky Mountain News.

The commotion destroyed the interview as the noise levels suddenly intensified and tables were knocked over and drinks spilled, all to the annoyance of the short tempered and infamous gambler.

"My God!... It's John L Sullivan," gawked the reporter.

"Eh?" Holliday's eyes did not distract from his whisky glass.

"John L Sullivan," the reporter repeated with noticeable fervor, "the one and only heavyweight champion of the whole world."

"Is there no God damn peace to be found in this shithole town?" Holliday exclaimed as the crowds now thronged to get near to the famous champion and encroach into his booth, knocking over his bottle of whisky in the melee.

Suddenly gunfire erupted and snowflake-like debris fell from the saloon ceiling. Everyone ducked, dived down low, or shielded their heads with their hands—everyone except Doc Holliday. He stood there in the immediate silence with the smoking LeMat pointing aloft.

"Now gentlemen. In the name of Christ, can we have some goddamn peace and quiet!" he announced with finality.

Cautiously, the bemused assembly began to rise from their knees, and parting bodies allowed the huge fighter to step through the congestion until he stood directly in front of Holliday.

"Do you mind exposing your theory of the need for gunfire here in the company of your fellow countrymen?" Looking down on the smaller thin man, Sullivan demanded an explanation.

"Thought we could all do with some peace and quiet… that's all." Despite his frail appearance, Holliday was still not afraid of anyone, especially when he had the LeMat by his side.

Sullivan frowned as he studied the delicate and pale-looking man standing before him.

"A man comes in here to relax and enjoy himself with a tipple or two," Holliday continued without hesitation, and he remained firm, with no fear on display as he explained his reasoning.

Unimpressed, Sullivan inched closer, moving his massive chest up against Holliday.

"I thought you maybe could do with a little breathing space from all the hurdy-gurdys and besides some low-down clumsy son of a bitch knocked my bottle over." Although avoiding eye contact, Holliday did not relent.

"Gentlemen… gentlemen," the news reporter cut in and wedged himself between the two men, sensing Holliday was soon to be the recipient of the famous hook. "Why don't you let me buy you a fresh bottle."

He spoke into Holliday's dull yellow eyes tentatively and placed his hand on Sullivan's back to try and usher him into the booth. "And please, Champ, why don't you join us?"

Knowing the great J. L. and the Doc were legendary for their yarn-telling and detecting a career-boosting, once-in-a-lifetime opportunity, he was not willing to allow this chance meeting to pass him by.

Without moving one inch, Sullivan's deep voice bellowed. "And you are?"

"Chester Brume… sir, of the Rocky Mountain News." Brume held out the palm of his hand to shake the champion's giant, famed right hand.

"It is very rare for anyone of note to visit Denver, let alone have two of America's finest in the same residence," he flattered.

Sullivan reluctantly accepted the greeting hand and, now curious due to the reporter's comments, returned his glare to the gun holder.

"And you, sir?"

"John Henry Holliday. Tired, hungry, drunk, and broke." Holliday released a slight presence of a grin.

"Doc… Doc… er, only the legendary Doc Holliday," Chester Brume added enthusiastically, stretching out his fingers to ease the pain in his hand from the vigorous handshake.

Sullivan took a slight step back to gain a better look at the wreck of a man in front of him.

"The Deadly Dentist?" Sullivan remarked, acknowledging he had heard of Holliday's fame and reputation.

"The one and only, Mr Sullivan," Brume nodded excitedly, "champion card shark and gunslinger, and now we have the heavyweight champion of the world side by side here in little old Denver."

This time he opened his arms and placed the flat of his hands on both Sullivan's and Holliday's backs as he centered them with subtle urgency.

"Please, gentlemen, sit. Come and please be seated," he urged them to join him at the table as his mind flooded with the prospect of the imminent scoop.

"Another bottle and fresh glasses," he shouted above the heads of the excited onlookers and toward the barman.

"I'll not refuse a drink paid for by one of my colleagues in the press." Sullivan was eager to hear first-hand accounts from the affable and admired legendary gunman, and he keenly lowered his massive frame into the booth.

Although lacking enthusiasm because he was no longer the most famous man in the room, Holliday quickly seated himself. Now he knew there was another bottle of whisky on its way.

"Get the photographer," Brume shouted to the nearest ears.

"There'll be no picture taking of me today," Holliday stated to Brume.

Sullivan scowled; he was not accustomed to people not wanting their photograph taken beside him, but said nothing.

Holliday was aware he did not look good, and appearing in print next to the fit brute opposite him would only increase his ailing appearance.

"Whatever you say, Doc," Brume appeased.
Knowing Holliday's notoriety for erratic mood swings and foul temper, he did not want to jeopardise the historic encounter.

"That's a fine-looking pistol you've got there, Mister Holliday," Sullivan commented as Holliday began to holster the LeMat.

"Indeed, sir, it is just that," Holliday returned a smile.

"It would surely look good in my collectibles," Sullivan nodded.

Holliday knew most people would be eager to please the champion, and they would be only too eager to offer him donations, but he was not fazed by being in the presence of someone so famous.

He was friends with Wyatt Earp, he had dined with Jesse James, and played faro with Billy the Kid, and so he remained unaffected by the subconscious concession that beset upon the ordinary folk, and he ignored the comment.

"Don't suppose you want to sell it?" Sullivan asked as Brume took to pouring out the drinks with a listening ear.

"Oh, I'm afraid not, sir," Holliday replied, almost as if he had been insulted. Brume held his poise and arched across the table with the whisky bottle in his grip as he listened.

"I'll give you a good price," Sullivan reached inside his coat and pulled out a well padded wallet. "The best price."

"I'm sorry, sir, but I will have to gratefully decline your very kind offer." Holliday raised his restocked shot glass to his lips.

"I assure you, Mr Sullivan, that I will take great care of it, and I will sit it nice and proper right next to my gold championship belt." By now, John L Sullivan had a hand full of one hundred dollar bills.

Holliday's narrow eyes enlarged and his mouth gaped at the sight of the fortune, but tapping the handle of the LeMat as if it was his faithful dog, he remained firm.

"It's not for sale, Mr Sullivan."

"Just name your price," he insisted, counting out notes flat on the table.

"The temptation of a cash windfall, Mr Sullivan, will not tempt me from parting with my long-time partner." Holliday slid his empty glass over to the now seated Brume to indicate a refill was required.

"One thousand… two thousand. Come on, Mr Holliday. Just name your price." Sullivan would not relent.

"I'm afraid, Mr Sullivan, we won't be parted. You see, me and my friend here have been through a hell of a lot together, and I fear we are inseparable until death. I guess these days it is the only thing I can rely upon." Holliday swigged off, in one gulp, the fresh spirit.

He felt someone dab his brow with a cold and damp cloth. He thought he could smell perfume, but he wasn't sure, because not long ago he thought he saw the shadow of Wyatt, but as he reached out, his old friend evaporated into the darkness.

His numbed senses were gradually waking, and dread began to spread from his bowels to his head, and it brought with it cold perspiration to his skin and desperation to his mind.

He drew a deep breath and held it for a moment as his mind allowed the acceptance of survival to gradually dissipate the happy remnants of the past.

His eyes flickered and cracked open to the light. Now he was sure he could smell the freshness of a woman near him, and he could feel the warmth of her breath as a face lowered down nearer to him for a closer inspection.

"Kate?" he rasped. "Is that you?"

"It's me, John. Just come to watch you pass over to hell." In keeping with the manner of their stormy relationship, Kate Elder could not resist returning to John Henry Holliday to witness in person the ending of his days.

Passionate love, propelled by destructive selfishness from both parties, had ensured the couple had fought, split, and reconciled regularly and repeatedly over the years. Now Kate knew there was to be no favourable finale with her husband, the dying gunman.

"That's my gal... always charged with compassion." He raised his finger towards a jug of stale water.

She paused and stared at his almost cadaverous frame, which had been ravaged by the life-ending disease.

"You'll get no sympathy from me, John. I'm just here to make sure you'll be cared for when you've gone," she replied, filling a tumbler and slanting the water to his dry, cracked lips.

"You know Wyatt called to see me last night." His face displayed a hint of pride.

"That's all you ever cared about."

She knew he had been hallucinating, and that he would have only seen the shadow of the man. "The God damn Earps," she blasted.

Although he wanted to talk about his friend, he knew it would only incense Kate's jealousy.

"I'm living on charity, Kate." The tepid water did little to ease the burning in his throat. "Ain't a dime to my name, so there'll be no grand shrine or celebrations." He started to cough.

"I always knew you'd end up with nothing but your worn-out boots," Kate pulled her head back from the ghastly odour of his breath.

Holliday coughed so hard it lifted his skeletal frame off the bed. He wheezed, and thick, dark green mucus, streaked with yellow pus, dripped from his mouth. His eyes began to water, and blood began to drip from his nose. His vision clouded, and he panted rapidly.

"Put a bullet in me, Kate, and end it," he whispered, knowing the effort of speech would induce yet more discomfort.

Kate did not reply. She arched away from the stench and drew fresh breath, then, composing herself, she dampened a cloth and wiped his face.

"End it for me now, Kate," again he pleaded.

"I wouldn't give you the pleasure of a swift and painless exit," Kate was still embittered by the wound he had inflicted upon her the last time she saw him, when his half-naked body was wrapped between the legs of a whore.

"I've suffered enough," he cried.

"You've not got long left, John… see it through to the end like a man. A real man, and not the fabled gunslinger which is in the daily prints."

"I'm begging you, Kate. Please end it. End it now." His tone was barely recognisable to Kate.

"Suffer, you lousy, no good asshole," Kate was resolute. "You're getting the ending you deserve."

"Think of the good times, Kate. Please don't let me die like this."

"I'm struggling to recall many." She had shed tears too often to feel any pity for the man who had troubled her for over a decade.

"Anyhow, God will collect you when he's ready," she turned away to avoid looking at him, "and in the manner you deserve."

Holliday tried to respond by opening his mouth, but the paralysing bouts of pain held him mute. He gritted his teeth and whispered,

"Please." He raised a trembling finger toward the LeMat on the bedside table and pointed. He was frightened, yet he felt strangely elated, sensing Kate's growing compassion and now the end was closing in around him.

Absorbed with tempting desire, Kate wrapped her trembling fingers around the walnut grip of the LeMat and released a pained, reminiscent smile.

Holliday clamped his eyes and began to pray.

Chapter 9

September 24th 1928

Thick windswept dust had been settling on Spangler's store for well over twelve months since old man Yeol Spangleberg had died alone in the storeroom of the business he built when the local businesses boomed and the town flourished.

The suspended sign above the door which once displayed 'Joe's Mercantile, Something for Everybody' now hung on a solitary rusty chain. The paint peeled; the weak sign was ready to crash to the floor with the next arriving gust of wind. The huge front window which once boasted an array of the finest supplies and collections of silver mining equipment was now slated over with nailed wooden planks, and only by pressing a single eye close between the narrow gaps was it able for anyone to see inside the dark store.

Long ago, the large square building was one of the first brick stores to be built in Denver after the fire of 1864, which reduced most of the commercial stores to blackened ash and charcoal. Old man Spangler came to Denver with his wife and small son in 1860, along with the other thousands of silver prospectors who invaded Denver and the neighbouring prosperous settlements intent on digging out their fortune.

After eighteen months of toil and little gain, Yoel Spangleberg decided to invest all his capital into a small supplies store on the corner of Larimer Street, where he sold everything from stoves to pickaxe handles and aprons to hobnail boots. Acting upon advice from another successful Jewish store owner in Aurora, he adopted the perceived non-religious name 'Joe Spangler' and his business thrived as Denver prospered.

But when the silver market collapsed in 1893 and the miners evacuated the region in droves, Spangler kept his business trading by moving into general mercantile and he bought and sold second-hand goods until eventually he became a full-time pawnbroker, with his store stocking and selling items from gold and silver jewellery to grand pianos.

As the years quickly passed by, Spangler's son left home to attend colleges and universities in faraway northern states, only returning on very special occasions and rare celebratory events, and he became more distant with every passing day until he was recalled by Joe as just an old memory.

Aya Spangleberg died after a fall and a long illness shortly after their young son left home, and so she left her husband Yoel alone and lonely with only his expansive but mainly worthless collection of once treasured loved pieces to occupy him and abate the years of loneliness.

Joe died alone and unnoticed until, after several days, one of the neighbouring shopkeepers forced his way through the rear door to find the body of the crumpled lifeless old man slumped in his reading chair.

Contact was made with Joseph Spangler Jr, but business commitments abroad prevented him from attending his father's funeral and taking care of his estate.

Now, twelve months later, Joseph Spangler Jr and his own two sons, Toby and Trent, had forced open the stiffened lock on the front door and entered the musty-smelling dark store. The dull tarnished doorbell only clanked; it did not ring as the door creaked inwards, allowing light to beam out brightly from the doorway and expose the contents of the building for the first time in over a year.

It was immediately obvious to Joe and the boys that the old man had become a hoarder who collected far more pieces than he sold, and finding a route through the stacks of boxes and piles of documents to the wall lamp proved difficult in the gloom.

A successful businessman, Joseph Spangler Jr, had originally chosen to pay a clearance company to register, sell, and auction off his father's entire miscellany.

He had no desire to return to his childhood hometown and stir up memories he would rather leave buried.

But after persistent pressure from his wife, who wanted him to spend more time with his sons, and from the boys themselves, who wanted to see their grandfather's store before it became nothing more than a reference number in the district accounts department, he finally relented.

He had called in at the old family home on the outskirts of town to ensure the marketing process was satisfactorily underway, but he chose not to stay there in the hollow shell and instead booked two rooms at the exclusive Grand Hotel in the central district of the city.

Scanning across the dusty mess, he was now regretting the concession, but he surmised at least he could use the opportunity to teach his boys some basic business accounting and finance principles.

He took up examining and logging items on the second floor, whilst Toby and Trent were instructed to inspect, wipe clean, log a description, and tag with a catalogue reference number each piece in the rear of the store.

Two days of clarifying and reconciling passed quickly for the boys but tediously slow for Joe, as the register list expanded with descriptions of jewellery, books, furniture, war medals, and other items, which enticed the insatiable curiosity of the boys.

Joe had spoken very little of his father to the boys and they knew almost nothing of his existence, and even now in his store very few questions were answered to the boys' bewilderment, but for fear of abruptly and prematurely ending the enlightening mini adventure they dared not probe too much into their grandpa's background.

The boys were not accustomed, nor at ease, to being in the company of their father. He worked abroad often, and for long periods, so they were schooled at boarding houses. They assumed their own father's relationship with their grandpa was also detached at a young age, but not wanting to risk a swift return to class, they quietly followed the precise and methodical instructions.

Toby squinted his eyes to stare at the last wooden crate, which was cornered at the rear of the racking. In the dark light, which was pierced by bright slanting shafts of light which penetrated through the boarded window, he could just see the crate had a stencil mark on the front. He stretched out and wiped the tips of his fingers across the grimy wood to reveal the red painted wording 'Old Irons'.

The box had been unattractive to Toby until now, and it was the last remaining crate on this rack.

He raised up on his toes and stretched out again to clamp his fingers onto the edge of the dust-laden lid. Slowly he began to drag the stubborn box to the front of the shelf and, with both hands, he lowered the heavy crate to the floor. He wiped the lid with his forearm and the dust made him sneeze repeatedly.

Again, the description 'Old Irons' was scribbled on the lid. With great force and leverage, Toby finally managed to crack open and then pull free the top.

"Holy shit!" he gushed to himself as his eyes fixed on the contents of the dark box.

"You say something down there?" Joe shouted down the stairwell.

"No, Pa. Just trapped my hand," Toby bluffed, not wanting to reveal to his father what he had found until he had inspected it with greater detail.

"You okay?"

"Yes, Pa. Just shocked me a little. That's all."

"Well, just be careful down there. You don't know what sort of junk is hidden away inside those boxes."

Toby slanted his head in the direction of the passageway and listened for movement.

Once satisfied his father was not coming down to investigate further, he drew in a long, cautious, but excited breath and slid his hand inside the dark box. Trent suspected Toby had found something interesting by his sudden discreet behaviour, so he paused and looked up from the clipboard.

When Toby did not call out the discovery for logging on the register, his hunch was confirmed.

Looking at Toby, he dropped the pencil and widened his eyes as he watched his older brother raise from the box a black pistol.

Trent scrambled immediately from the comfort of the worn-out leather couch to kneel at his brother's side. He too peered inside the box and, after a brief moment, he dropped his hand inside the dark hollow to feel the sharp coldness of the metal. He reached down and felt around until he grasped his small fingers around a handle, then he too lifted out an old pistol.

Both boys inspected the heavy guns carefully, their imaginations giving rise to legendary adventures and daring escapades.

Trent needed to use both hands to hold level the pistol as he practiced aiming at a coat stand and then a jardinière whilst Toby dragged the box into a shaft of light so that he could better see the half dozen or so pistols which had been locked away for many years.

"What's going on down there, boys? I can't hear much inventory taking going on." So absorbed in their fantasies, the brothers had not heard the approach of their father's footsteps on the wooden floorboards above.

"What in the darn nation have you got there?" Even in the oily yellow partial light, he knew what they were both holding aloft, so his question was more of an observation.

Fearing a stern rebuke, the brothers simultaneously dropped the pistols back into the box, which had been their home for many a year. A loud clatter sounded as metal slammed against metal, but no one spoke and the boys remained rigid and dared not move as Joe approached. They feared a severe scolding and a lengthy lecture, but ignoring the small reddening faces, Joe gazed into the deep blackness of the container at his feet, his face revealing an unexpected pleasurable distraction from what had become a tedious monotony.

He placed his pencil above his ear, lowered down, and extended his hand inside the box, allowing his fingers to slide across the metal and from one pistol to another until his hand settled upon an engraved barrel that intrigued him. Raising the LeMat, he cupped both hands around its cold body and paced nearer to the wall lantern.

"What a beauty," he surprisingly exclaimed. "Well, boys, something of interest at last."

"Yeah, Pa. What is it?" asked Trent.

"I've no idea, but it sure is different from anything I've seen before." He angled the LeMat to catch the light of the oil lamp.

"You think it's valuable?" The boys inquisitively neared their father.

"Doubt it, boys, but it sure is special."

He studied the decorative etching, which was now solid black with years of hardened grime.

He flipped it over and looked at the dried-out walnut handle, then rolled the barrel, which still spun with ease.

"Do you think it belongs to anyone famous?" Trent looked up toward his towering father.

"Well, you old rascal," he unintentionally ignored the boys and muttered to himself. "Guns in your precious store."

"Jesse James!" beamed Toby.

"Who would have thought it?" Joe was momentarily distracted.

His thoughts cast back to a time when he was a child, and his backside was beaten raw.

He had been play-acting with a broom handle and his father caught him aiming the shaft as a makeshift rifle. Admonishing his son because he did not approve of weapons, Yeol took to beating his son hard with a leather strap until Joe Junior pledged he would never mimic gunplay again.

Much later, Joe learned from his mother that his father's younger brother had been killed by a stray bullet whilst he was on an errand delivering groceries to a neighbour.

"Billy the Kid!" Trent smiled with wild imagination.

"Doubt it, boys." Joe's attention was brought back to the present. "No one of any notoriety has ever been out to these parts." Still, he did not remove his gaze from the neglected, but still striking LeMat. "Probably just been left in this old box doing nothing all these years."

He rolled the LeMat over again and tried to read the serial number, which was barely visible on the cylinder. "Er 4…2, 8. Even has a serial number."

"Does that mean anything, Pa?"

"Doubt it. I guess they all have a marker of some kind." He considered going out of the store and into the brightness so that he could improve his view, but he dismissed the idea because he wanted to finish the register as soon as possible and return home.

Finally, he flipped onto his palm the small paper tag which was fastened by string to the trigger guard. The small card read in faded pencil: '4th Nov 1887. K. ELDER. $10.'

"Er, K…K…Kelder," he misread the name to the boys. "There you go. This was owned by some fellow named Kelder."

He glanced down at the two disappointed faces. "Ever heard of him, boys?"

"Nope. Have you?" Together the boys disappointedly shook their heads.

"Never."

"Maybe we could ask around town? Someone may remember a Kelder," hankered Toby.

He badly wanted to trace the owner. He still held on to imaginations of the gun belonging to some notorious outlaw.

"We haven't got time to waste on wild goose chases," Joe dismissed, eager to get the work completed and return home.

"Are you going to keep it?" wished Toby.

"No… no, Toby. It's probably worthless and I have no desire to possess any such weaponry." He extended his hand in his son's direction and noticed the boy's excitement deflate. "Here, log it with the rest and we will get the auctioneers to investigate the finer details for the sale."

He placed the LeMat into the small accepting hand and then hurried back upstairs to continue with the registry.

Only a few moments had passed when Joe heard an explosion, followed immediately by a thud from the room below him. His eyes widened with alarm and his heart swelled with innate fear. He rushed down the stairwell, jumping clear of the final steps, and burst into the acrid, smoke-filled room to see a pallid-faced Trent trembling before him.

"He was just looking at it, Pa," he stammered as tears erupted and flooded down from his wide-open eyes.

Trepidation consumed Joe's every fibre and slowly, with an assumed dread for what he suspected, he stretched his neck and looked where Toby had stood only moments earlier.

Blood and brains were splattered across the low ceiling and the far wall.

He dared not move, but as the cloud of smoke swirled, he saw Toby's quivering body lying face down in an enlarging pool of blood. His blonde hair was spiked at the back and it was matted with red and bone fragments. On the floorboards next to his small hand was the smoking LeMat.

Joe dropped to his knees and screamed until vomit clogged his throat.

Chapter 10

24th September 1919

The 15.30 overnighter from Denver to Union Station, Chicago rocked and rumbled as it sped along the four-foot gauge across the wide open empty flats of Kansas.

Bruno 'The Slayer' Carlini gazed out of the huge clear window of his private sleeper cabin. He rested his shoulder against the glass, but he could see nothing in the empty blackness except the imperfect reflection of his recently acquired LeMat and his self-assured, but serene countenance. Although ten hours into the journey, he had not removed his black trench coat, fedora, or leather gloves, and so only the LeMat and his face caught the dim carriage light and returned the reflection.

He cradled the LeMat tightly in his lap, his thoughts occupied with Big Jim Colosimo's rapidly approaching fortieth birthday party. Only Colosimo's immediate family and most senior and trusted associates were invited to participate in the extravagance. Honoured, but not without good reason, Carlini had been selected to be seated to the right of his boss, who was normally only flanked by his blood family.

Power fever obsessed Carlini's mind, and he knew he would be the envy of all of Chicago's underworld when he presented the LeMat to Colosimo as a birthday gift.

Carlini's mouth curled, causing a small crease in one of his cheeks as the thought of pleasing the feared mobster boss exhilarated him.

Before leaving Denver, he had wired ahead to one of his accomplices in Chicago with restoration instructions and the sourcing of six round-cut diamonds which he wanted studded into each side of the walnut handle. This costly additional touch was considered a vital investment by Carlini because he knew Colosimo favoured wearing ostentatious diamonds.

Big Jim Colosimo had a renowned reputation for displaying his wealth in his jewellery, and Carlini knew Colosimo would be impressed by the dazzling additions.

He was well aware loathing jealousy would also give rise to and expose him to peril from the other Capos who wanted to improve their position and status within Colosimo's ranks, but he knew by securing the favour of Colosimo he would be protected and would not be the ignorant victim of a bullet in the back of his head.

Bruno Carlini had grown up fast and mean in Little Italy, Chicago.

Fatherless from the age of six, he lived within walking distance of Death Corner on St Cleveland Street, and so most of his youth was spent either witnessing or being involved in criminal activities which were best undertaken under the cover of darkness.

He was a much larger-than-average boy compared to his Italian friends in the neighbourhood. He had huge hands, an enormous barrelled chest, and he was fleet of foot.

He excelled in wrestling and boxing and could have furthered a successful career in either of the combat sports, but he chose to enter into illegal enterprises instead of attending after-school training sessions. He ran errands, collected debts, and delivered the notorious black notes for his uncles, who supplemented their earnings with protection money.

When there was trouble from the Irish boys at the end of the block, Carlini was the first boy his friends would call upon and, as he entered his adolescence, his notoriety was renowned throughout the area.

He grew up with a mean, callous, and unforgiving nature, and his violence had no limits. He developed into a ruthless, huge man with no fear, and he was no stranger to violent ways.

He knew how to get what he wanted and he had the means, body tools, and techniques to ensure he got it.

For over ten years, developing from a teenage menace into a contract killer, he worked his way through the strict code and ranks of the Italian underworld.

In the early years, he assisted with rent collections, racketeering, and extortion and, after proving his loyalty within the 'family', he was enlisted as a soldier.

Now his duties were elevated to a more sinister level. In these dangerous times, no other name was more feared than Bruno Carlini.

Performing his duties without inviting any unwanted suspicions, Bruno Carlini soon became known as 'The Slayer' by the mobster accomplices who respected him, but in private he was called 'Merda Pala' by those who envied him. The nickname Merda Pala, or "shit shoveller", stuck because he became renowned for being called upon to clear up the mess of other less competent assassins.

Eventually, because of the unequalled quality of his work and his true Italian blood lineage, he received the reward he had been seeking, and he was promoted to the rank of Capo where he would report to, and receive orders directly from Chicago's only Mafia boss, Big Jim Colosimo, whose empire and wealth had rapidly spread as he infested the disease of crime into Chicago's economic prosperity.

The Slayer was now at his peak, and he felt invincible. He recalled with pride his invitation to meet the boss for the first time. He was told to dress up in his best shirt and suit as he would be dining out and he recalled his pulse racing as he was blindfolded and taken to an address which was unknown to him.

He was seated alone at a large oval table in a semi-lit empty restaurant and when the covering was removed he was left momentarily until a dozen black-clad gangsters entered the room and silently seated themselves around the oval leaving just one empty chair next to him.

Red wine was poured and copious amounts of piping hot pasta and meatball dishes were distributed until finally, Big Jim Colosimo entered the room.

Again silence fell, and the eating was paused as Colosimo, who was flanked by two bodyguards, lowered himself into the only empty chair next to Carlini.

Colosimo nodded his approval and the two heavies took a few steps back and positioned themselves at his rear with their backs straight against the wall and their eyes locked upon the diners. Colosimo raised his glass and proposed a toast and then the supper recommenced.

More toasts followed and oaths were recited throughout the evening and after the food was consumed, Colosimo sliced the palm of his right hand and instructed Carlini to do the same, then they rubbed their palms together to pledge a blood bond.

This was when Carlini had relaxed enough to notice Colosimo's passion for diamonds. His fingers were covered with heavy gold rings, all of which were highly decorated with huge gleaming stones, as was his tie pin, cufflinks, and glasses.

More promises of loyalty were made and finally, Carlini was asked to hold a burning piece of paper that contained the sacred words of the Mafia pledge.

Finally, once the initiation was completed to Colosimo's satisfaction, the rest of the evening blurred away with the consumption of vintage Italian red, Roman brandy, and the strict omission of any business talk.

Carlini knew at that moment he would one day honour 'Diamond' Jim Colosimo with respect and gratitude by presenting him with a very special gift that none of his fellow associates around the table could equal.

That day was now approaching and 'The Slayer' felt triumphant. Thirty hours earlier, the immaculately clad American Italian had checked into the lavish Hubert Hotel.

Attired in the finest Italian pin-striped fabric with black, reflective, shining shoes combined with his deep-set piercing eyes and jet pompadour hair, the huge man stood out from the rest of the assembly.

Most of the gathered had descended upon the Hubert in preparation for Theodore Winkfield's monthly auction, which was commencing in the public forum house across the street at ten am the following morning.

Famed for its extravagant collections, Winkfield's auctions attracted bidders and buyers from far beyond the borders of Colorado.

Bruno Carlini had often trawled through the small print of adverts and auction notices looking for rarities and was thrilled when he read the notification for catalogue number 81: 'An 1860s LeMat revolver with serial number 428' in Winkfield's auction catalogue to which he subscribed.

He had no knowledge that four months earlier the Spangler family, consumed by grief, had abandoned their inventory register and called in clearance professionals to sell off old man Spangler's property and stock and put to auction any items of potential worth or significant interest.

The aging LeMat had fallen into this category and with viewing now closed, the bidding was envisaged to commence around lunchtime tomorrow.

With an immense knowledge and passion for handheld killing machines, Carlini did not need to satisfy his curiosity with a viewing. He knew its worth and what he was prepared to pay, and once in his ownership he knew exactly who to contact back in Chicago to ensure the LeMat would be restored back to its full glory with the addition of the very expensive enhancements.

Denver had bored Carlini quickly. After his evening meal, he walked to the entertainment district, but nothing aroused him and he sought to end the night with a glass of red in the hotel bar before he retired for an early night.

He stood alone with his elbow folded on the dark polished wooden bar and his right foot resting on the brass foot rail. His eyes were slanted down towards his almost empty glass and he was minding his own business with his thoughts concentrating upon business in Chicago when he was alerted by comments made nearby.

Suddenly he was interested in one of the two businessmen who stood five feet to his left. A loud southern braggart was making it no secret to anyone who was prepared to listen for a few moments that he was also in Denver to purchase the LeMat.

His words were slurred and affected by excessive alcohol, but their meaning was clear to all who listened. Overdressed to stand out from the other drinkers like a peacock, he offered out free drinks to anyone who was prepared to adopt a friendly ear for a few moments and listen to his self-praise of tracking down a LeMat and his self-assured belief that by lunchtime tomorrow he would be the proud owner of the rare Civil War memorabilia. Funds being of little concern to him, he had displayed wealth, and he extravagantly flaunted it to all with his fancy attire and his flippant attitude for spending cash.

"Rack 'em up," he commanded, without turning to address the barman.

"Excuse me, sir?" The bartender turned from his waist to face the caller. He had been wiping glasses and did not fully hear the call.

"You heard me, boy!" The braggart snarled.

"Sorry." The barman continued to replace glasses on the rack behind the bar.

"I said rack 'em up." This time the order was followed with a clatter of glass as the man slid both his and his companion's whisky glasses along the bar.

"Are you celebrating, sir?" The barman asked.

"Mind your own and just do as you're told," he slurred. "Same again for me and Mister Malloch here." He then swivelled his head in both directions of the bar and added loudly, "Yeah, I'm celebrating."

This time no one purposely paid him any attention and so his eyes rested upon the whisky refill.

"Good health and good luck to you, Mister Degar." Malloch raised his glass almost before the bartender had finished pouring.

"I don't need good luck or any darn luck at all. The LeMat is mine already and I'm celebrating." Degar also snatched at his glass and downed it in one gulp. "Rack 'em up again." He bellowed at the barman before he could refit the bottle stopper.

"Whatever you say." The barman replied with a hint of reluctance, which Degar noted.

"Now shut your God-darn mouth!" Dager spat once the glass was refilled. "And get back to your business."

He then tossed a five-dollar bill in the barman's direction. "And stuff this in it. It might help you to keep quiet."

The barman ignored both the slander and money and turned his back to continue with his duties. Dager's face released an uncontrolled smirk, and he again looked around to seek attention, but he saw only one other person within earshot.

"Hey fella." He shouted over his right shoulder, but the big man's eyes remained centred on his glass.

"Hey there." Dager turned his head fully and slurred. "Yeah, you." Carlini raised an eyebrow towards the drunk. "I'm talking to you. You wanna join us for a drink?"

"No, but thank you." Carlini dismissed the offer by holding out the flat of his hand.

"I'm celebrating." Degar held aloft his tumbler.

"Oh yeah." Carlini led.

"Yes sir. I sure am." His whisky-reddened face beamed with presumption. "Come tomorrow, I'm going to be getting myself a LeMat." He set, parading a huge grin.

"A what?" Carlini bluffed.

"A LeMat!" Degar's forehead lined and his eyes narrowed. "You know. The famous Civil War gun."

Carlini finished off his red wine and shook his head. "Never heard of it."

"You're joshing with me," Dager fixed his eyes to focus on the man, then he slurped from the glass. "Ain't you?"

Then he fully turned to face Carlini front on.

"Nope. I never heard of such a gun." The relaxed Italian replied, feigning any interest.

"Come on," Dager's eyebrows lined with disbelief. "You must have."

"Uh?" Malloch spun on his stool to support Dager. "Everybody I know has heard of the most famous Civil War revolver."

"Well, not where I'm from, they ain't."

"Urr… ignoramus." Malloch spat, turning back to face the display of shiny bottles which interested him more.

"Le… what. What you call it." Carlini feigned.

"LeMat. Issued to Confederate generals and such like only." Degar smiled.

"So what makes you so sure?" Carlini asked.

"So sure. So sure of what?" Now Degar's face slanted to one side and the presuming smile was replaced with gaping perplexity. "You're going to get the gun."

"Ah, I see." Degar's liquor-befuddled mind was finding it difficult to understand the question, and he was slow to respond. "Because I'm prepared to pay top dollar and go all the way…… Yes, sir, I will not allow anyone to stop me now. I've been trying to get hold of one of these for years."

Degar emptied his glass by pouring the burning liquid down his throat.

"Fill 'em up," he motioned with his loose arm to the barman indicating a refill, "and one for my new friend here."

"No. No, thank you."

"Ah, come over here and celebrate with me. I've been after a LeMat for years and I want to share my success."

"Sorry, I've got an early start."

Carlini turned over his glass and placed it on the counter rim down to confirm he was finished.

"Well then, cigars all round." Degar was persistent. "Join me for a smoke before you retire." He rummaged in his pocket for notes and tossed them out onto the bar.

"No thanks. As I said, I've got an early start."

Carlini saw Degar's key fob amongst the crumpled green notes on the bar and he noted the number, thirty one.

"What? You won't smoke with me."

As with most drunks, the declined offer was received as an insult.

"What's wrong with my hospitality?"

"Nothing…… just tired, that's all."

"You sure?" Degar shouted. "Because suddenly I'm thinking that my company and my money ain't good enough for you!"

The drunk considered himself superior to the olive-skinned man leant a few yards away and his bias perceived the decline as an insult.

"Am I right?"

"Not at all. I've been travelling all day long and I'm ready for hitting the sack. That's all." Carlini remained calm.

"Come on now, Mr Dager." The bartender leant closer. "Please lower your voice. We have other customers in here tonight."

"Shut it, you! I've told you once to keep your filthy black mouth shut."

Carlini firmed the fedora into position and pulled the brim low to shadow his scheming eyes. He found it challenging not to put his fist in the southern windbag's mouth, so he tensed up, his body rigid, and drew a long calming breath.

He did not want to draw any unwanted attention from the local law and he chose to remain anonymous. His intentions were to simply purchase the LeMat and get in and out of Denver unnoticed, as soon as he could.

"Good evening, sir." Bid the tender.

Carlini nodded a smile in return and turned towards the door.

"What the hell is wrong with these dago bastards? They crawl out of their slums and think they own the whole bloody country," Degar shouted in Carlini's direction.

"Ah, he's just a coward," Malloch appeased, easing Dagar back onto his stool.

The slayer did not take the doorway which opened the way to his room on level two; instead, he continued up the stairwell and turned on the corridor which led to level three.

He knew the loudmouths would not match their drunken bravado with any knuckle action, but still he kept his footsteps silent on the dark planks, occasionally glancing over his shoulder to ensure no one was following behind in the gloom.

He stopped at room number thirty one and again looked left and right along the corridor and, satisfied the passage was clear of prying suspicious eyes, he reached inside his trench pocket and pulled out a needle file. Within seconds he was behind the door of thirty one. He quickly scanned across the small undisturbed room and saw Dager's brown leather travel case laid on its side, where he had excitedly dropped it in his haste to access the hotel bar.

Although Carlini's interest was not roused enough to search the room or Dager's belongings, he quietly pulled out and tipped the bedside drawers, spilt open the thick leather case, and turned out and scattered across the floor the contents.

He was determined and intent on leaving the room without clues or signs of his identity, so he silently created a break-in and robbery scene by opening the window and turning out the drawers and the contents of Degar's case.

He sat quietly in the dark for over two hours with his mind focused on the task ahead. His hands did not tremble, nor did his legs quiver. He was an expert lifetaker who did his best work under the shroud of darkness.

It was in the early hours of the morning when Carlini heard heavy cumbersome footsteps accompanied by the loud clopping of high heels approaching beyond the room door.

Slurred speech and high-pitched giggling grew louder as the pair of drunks neared room thirty one. The morning daylight had yet to lift the dimness within the hotel and, other than the approach of a man and a woman, the hotel was noiseless.

Carlini slithered into position behind the hinges of the door and withdrew his antique Solingen cutthroat from within his sock. He drew in a deep breath and listened to the key rattling noisily in the lock. He had not anticipated the drunk would bring back a whore for company, but he was not unduly concerned. He knew he had the advantage of surprise and speed, and once aligned with his skills of destruction, the outcome was inevitable.

After a few clumsy attempts to open the door, a weak spray of orange from the corridor lamp shone a gauzy beam into the entrance of the unlit room.

"Oh, Max, are you going to be in for a treat tonight," the whore teased in Degar's ear as he squinted in the doorway to let his eyes adjust to the darkness. Linking arms and leaning on each other, they staggered slowly forward.

Degar half turned to shut out the light by slamming the door, but his legs almost buckled and he had to support himself by grabbing tight both the door handle and the whore's pearl-coloured flapper.

As the latch clicked, Carlini flashed his blade across the whore's throat and simultaneously clasped his left arm around Dager's neck, locking his gloved hand tight across his drooling mouth.

Then he reached out his right hand to grasp firmly the whore's sagging body and lower the dying woman to the floor.

"Yeah Max. You're in for a real treat tonight," Carlini whispered as he sliced the blade across Dager's throat, severing it deep through the muscle and from ear to ear. "Courtesy of the dago bastard."

Carlini's black leather gloves ensured he did not feel the gush of gurgling blood, but he pulled back slightly when a geyser of hot blood spurted diagonally across his face and blurred his vision. However, unaffected by the hot liquid, he calmly held Degar firm and guided his wilting body to the bedside commode.

Degar did not see or hear his murderer, and he was too drunk to understand he had taken his last breath. He sucked in air through the enormous laceration and his organs frantically pulsated to survive. His eyes gaped wide with involuntary alarm, but he could see nothing and his scrambled mind failed to digest that death was approaching fast.

Carlini manoeuvred the ailing body into the chair and Degar's lifeless head dropped with his chin resting on his deflated chest. He then wiped clean the Solingen across the dead man's shoulder and then he refolded the blade to replace the razor within his sock. Dabbing the blood from his face with his silk handkerchief, he felt inside Degar's jacket and removed a note-bulging wallet. He paused for a moment to listen at the room door for any concerning noises beyond, but once satisfied Degar had been eliminated successfully, he carefully stepped over the whore and her pooling blood to quietly exit the room.

He placed the 'Do Not Disturb' sign on the door handle and, confident the only obstacle blocking him from purchasing the LeMat had been removed, he disappeared into the hazy dimness, assured that he could make the purchase of the LeMat and be well out of Denver before the two blood-drained bodies were discovered.

Carlini broke his pensive gaze away from the black but reflecting train window and released a satanic fulfilled smile. Almost as if for reassurance, he stroked the prized steel in his lap whilst his mind conjured up pulsing visions of accommodating desirous women, dance music, beef Carpaccio, and Big Jim Colosimo's beaming smile of gratification as his huge hands received the diamond-studded and refurbished LeMat from his latest favourite Capo.

March 15th 2016

In 2016 a LeMat revolver was sold at Barneby's auction for $224,250.

The character Levi Clayton features in 'The Vengeance Trail' and 'The Return'.

Other titles by Daniel Carlson include;

The Apostle

A Kiss for the Cursed

The Vengeance Trail

The Return

The Life and Death of My Best Friend, Davy Crockett

The Highwayman and the Spy

The Highwayman and the Prince

The Boy, a Dog and the Great War

The Betrayal

The Highwayman. The factual and historical novelization of John Nevison's life

The Battle of Flamborough Head

The Badge and the Bullet